The Cabinet-Maker and Upholsterer's Companion

Stokes, J

Copyright © BiblioLife, LLC

This historical reproduction is part of a unique project that provides opportunities for readers, educators and researchers by bringing hard-to-find original publications back into print at reasonable prices. Because this and other works are culturally important, we have made them available as part of our commitment to protecting, preserving and promoting the world's literature. These books are in the "public domain" and were digitized and made available in cooperation with libraries, archives, and open source initiatives around the world dedicated to this important mission.

We believe that when we undertake the difficult task of re-creating these works as attractive, readable and affordable books, we further the goal of sharing these works with a global audience, and preserving a vanishing wealth of human knowledge.

Many historical books were originally published in small fonts, which can make them very difficult to read. Accordingly, in order to improve the reading experience of these books, we have created "enlarged print" versions of our books. Because of font size variation in the original books, some of these may not technically qualify as "large print" books, as that term is generally defined; however, we believe these versions provide an overall improved reading experience for many.

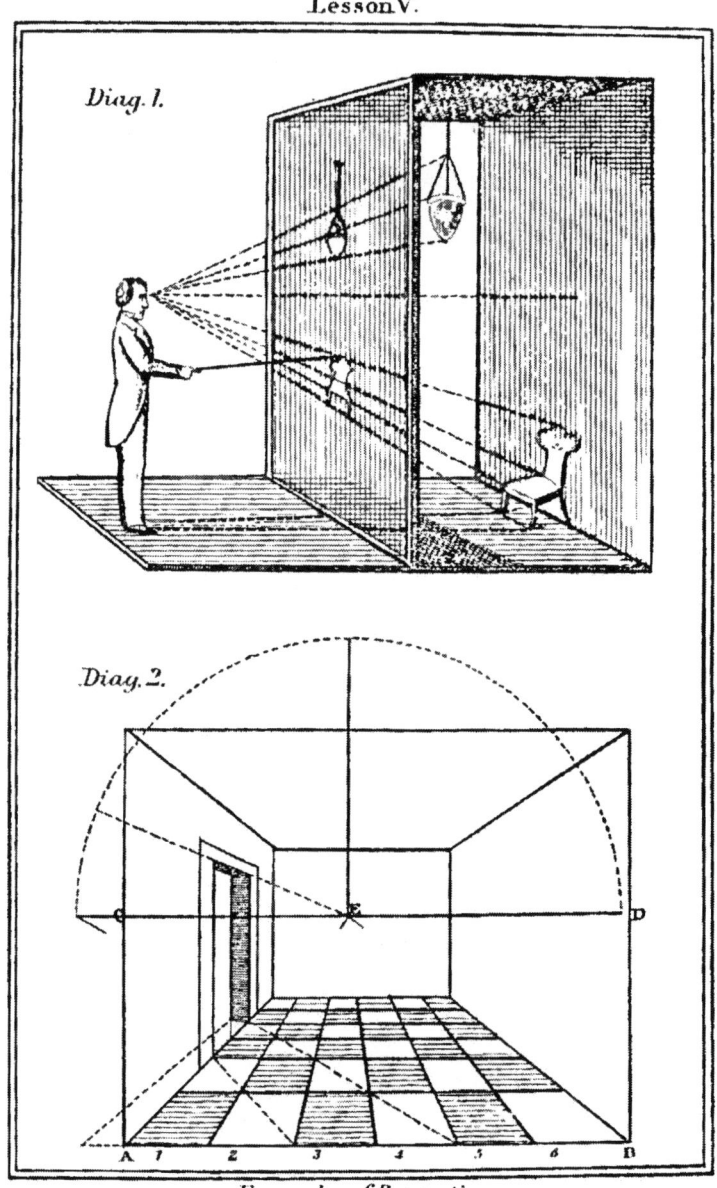

Examples of Perspective

THE

CABINET-MAKER

AND

UPHOLSTERER'S COMPANION:

COMPRISING

THE ART OF DRAWING,
AS APPLICABLE TO CABINET WORK;
VENEERING, INLAYING, AND BUHL-WORK;
THE ART OF DYEING AND STAINING WOOD, IVORY,
BONE, TORTOISE-SHELL, ETC.
DIRECTIONS FOR LACKERING, JAPANNING,
AND VARNISHING;
TO MAKE FRENCH POLISH, GLUES, CEMENTS, AND
COMPOSITIONS;
WITH NUMEROUS RECEIPTS,
USEFUL TO WORKMEN GENERALLY.

BY J. STOKES.

ILLUSTRATED.

A NEW EDITION, WITH AN APPENDIX UPON FRENCH POLISHING
STAINING, IMITATING, VARNISHING, ETC., ETC.

PHILADELPHIA:
HENRY CAREY BAIRD & CO.,
INDUSTRIAL PUBLISHERS, BOOKSELLERS, AND IMPORTERS,
810 WALNUT STREET.
1904.

CONTENTS.

INTRODUCTION.

PART I.

ORNAMENTAL CABINET MAKING.

	PAGE
THE RUDIMENTS OF DRAWING AS APPLICABLE TO ARTICLES OF FURNITURE.	13
PRIMARY OBSERVATIONS ON DRAWING ORNAMENTS FOR CABINET WORK.	18
GEOMETRICAL AND PERSPECTIVE TERMS, DEFINED AND EXPLAINED	21
Geometry	23
Perspective	24
The Rudiments of Shadowing.	28
The Rudiments of Coloring	31
To Imitate Mahogany, Rosewood	32
To imitate Satin Wood, Bronze, Brass, Ormolu, Velvet, Green Baize, Glass, Porphyry Marble, Verd-Antique Sienna Marble, Mona Marble.	33
To Imitate Black Marble, Buff Color Drapery, White Drapery, Chintz, Gilt Poles, Crimson Curtains, Painted Landscapes	34
ORNAMENTS USED IN CABINET WORK—THEIR TERMS EXPLAINED.	36
Foliage Ornament, Mixed Ornament.	36
Festooned Ornament, Arabesque Ornament, Winding Foliage, Serpentine or Running Ornament, Plaited Ornament,	37
Guilloche Ornament, Fret Ornament, Mosaic Ornament, Buhl Ornament	38
ORNAMENTS USED IN CABINET AND UPHOLSTERING WORK—WHEN AND WHERE MOST APPLICABLE	88

PART II.

VENEERING, INLAYING, ETC.

OF VENEERING	45
Gluing and Veneering as Applied to Card and Other Table Tops, Secretary and Book Case Fronts, etc.	46
To Raise old Veneers.	47
A Strong Glue well Suited for Inlaying of Veneering; To Veneer Tortoise Shell	48
BUHL WORK	49
To Prepare Shell or Brass Ready for Cutting Out; Cutting Out the Pattern	50

(iii)

iv CONTENTS.

	PAGE
To Glue up the Patterns	51
Laying your Veneer	52
Inlaying with Shaded Wood	53
To Imitate Inlaying of Silver Strings, etc.	54
A Glue for Inlaying Brass or Silver Strings; To Polish Brass Ornaments Inlaid in Wood; to Wash Brass Figures Over with Silver; To Imitate Tortoise Shell on Copper	55

PART III.

DYEING, STAINING. GILDING, ETC.

DYEING Fine Black; Another Method	58
Fine Blue	59
Another Blue; a Fine Yellow	60
A Bright Yellow, Liquid for Brightening and Setting Colors; A Bright Green	61
Another Green; Bright Red; Another Red	62
Purple; Another Purple	63
Orange; Silver Grey	64
Another Grey	65
STAINING	65
Black Staining for Immediate Use; To Stain Beach a Mahogany Color; Another Method for a Black Stain	66
To Imitate Rosewood	67
To Imitate King or Botany Bay Wood; Red Stain for Bedsteads and Common Chairs; to improve the color of any stain	68
To Stain Horn in Imitation of Tortoise Shell; to Stain Ivory or Bone Red	69
To Stain Ivory or Bone Black, Green, Blue, Yellow	70
To Stain Musical Instruments, Fine Crimson, Purple, Fine Black	71
Fine Blue, Fine Green, Bright Yellow, to Stain Box Wood Brown	72
Silvering and Gilding	73
The Requisites Necessary to be Provided with; Size for Oil Gilding	74
To Make Size for Preparing Frames, etc.; to Prepare Frames or Wood Work	75
Polishing	76
Gold Size, Another Gold Size, to Prepare your Frames for Gilding	77
Laying on the Gold	78
Burnishing	79
Matting or Dead Gold; Finishing	80
To Make Shell Gold. Silver Size, Silvering	81
To Make Liquid Foil for Silvering Glass Globes, Bent Mirrors, etc.	82
Excellent Receipt to Burnish Gold-size, to Gild Leather for Bordering-doors, Folding Screens, etc.	83
To Gild the Borders of Leather Tops of Library Tables, etc.	84
Bronzing, to Bronze Figures	85
To Bronze on Wood	86
To Bronze Brass Figures for Ornaments	87

CONTENTS.

PART IV.

LACKERING, JAPANNING, VARNISHING, ETC.

	PAGE
LACKERING. To Lacquer Brass Work	88
To Make Gold Lackers for Brass	89
Superior Lacker for Brass; Pale Gold Lacker; Lacker with Spirits of Turpentine	90
To Clean Old Brass Work for Lackering	91
JAPANNING	92
A Black Japan; To Imitate Black Rosewood	93
India Japanning	94
Grounds for Chinese Japan	95
To Make Black Japan; to Trace your Designs on the Ground; to Raise Figures on Your Work	96
Bronzes Peculiarly Adapted for India Japanning and Similar Purposes; Gold	97
Copper, Silver	98
Tin, Method of Applying the Bronze	99
To Japan Work Boxes, etc.	100
Ceiling Wax Varnish	101
VARNISHING	102
Cautions Respecting the Making of Varnish	103
General Directions in Choosing Gums and Spirits	104
To Varnish a Piece of Furniture	105
To Make the Best White Hard Varnish; to Keep Brushes in Order	106
Mastic Varnish for Pictures or Drawings, Turpentine Varnish, Varnishes for Violins, etc.	107
To Varnish Drawings, or any Kind of Paper or Card Work	108
Amber Varnish; Oil Varnish	109
Copal Varnish; to Make a Colorless Copal Varnish	110
Turpentine Copal Varnish	111
A Varnish Which Suits all Kinds of Prints and Pictures; to Make Appear in Gold the Figures of a Print	112
Method of Preparing the Composition Used for Colored Drawings and Prints, to Make Them Resemble Paintings in Oil; Polishing	113
To Polish Varnish; the French Method of Polishing	114
To Polish Brass Ornaments Inlaid in Wood; to Polish Ivory; to Polish Pearl	115
To Polish Marble; To Polish Tortoise Shell or Horn	116
Friction Varnishing, or French Polishing	117
The True French Polish	118
Another French Polish	119
An Improved Polish; Water-proof Polish	120
Bright Polish; Prepared Spirits	121
Strong Polish; Directions for Cleansing and Polishing Old Furniture	122

PART V.

GLUES, CEMENTS, ETC.

CEMENTS. To Make Mahogany Colored Cement; Portable Glue, or Bank Note Cement	123
Cement for Turners; a Cement for Broken Glass	124
A Cement to Stop Flaws or Cracks in Wood of any Color; Cements for Joining China, etc.	125

CONTENTS.

	PAGE
A Strong Glue that will Resist Moisture	126
Another Glue that will Resist Moisture; Paste for Laying Cloth or Leather on Table Tops	127
MISCELLANEOUS RECEIPTS. Glass Paper	129
To Clean the Face of Soft Mahogany or Other Porous Wood	130
To Darken Light Mahogany	131
To Cut Good Steel Scrapers; to Sharpen and Set a Saw	132
To Take Bruises out of Furniture	133
To Make Anti-attrition; Polish for Turner's Work	134
To Clean and Restore the Elasticity of Cane Chair Bottoms, etc.; to Clean Silver Furniture; to Clean Marble, Sienna, Jasper, Porphyry, or Scagalio	135
To Take Ink Spots out of Mahogany; to Make Furniture Paste	136
To Make Furniture Oil; Black Wax	137
Green Wax; to Take out Spots of Oil or Grease from Cloth; to Make Parchment Transparent	138
To Take Out Wax Spots from Cloth or Silk; to Soften and to Bleach Ivory	139
To Solder or Weld Tortoise Shell or Horn; to Clean Carpets or Tapestry; to Make Composition Ornaments for Picture Frames, etc	140
To Clean Pictures	141
To Clean Pictures; to Silver Clock Faces, etc	142
Varnish for Clock Faces, etc	143
Crystallized Tin; to render Plaster Figures Very Durable	144
To Make Transparent or Tracing Paper	145
To Gild Metal by Dissolving Gold in Aqua-regia; to Silver Ivory	146
To Clean Mirrors, Ormolu Ornaments, etc	147
A Green Paint; to Preserve Wood Against Injury from Fire	148
To Remove Stains in Tables; Hints in Melting and Using Glue; to Renew a Polished Surface; to Clean off the Surface of Solid Work	149
To Clean Lackered Work in Brass Furniture; to Cast Ornaments, etc., to Resemble Wood	150
Cement Stopping	151
To Clean a Veneered Surface; Grease or Dirt in French Polish; Choice of Tools	152
To Temper Saws, Chisels, etc	154

APPENDIX.

Wood Staining, Washing	156
Matching	157
Improving	158
Painting	159
Imitations	160
Directions for Staining	163
Sizing and Embodying	164
Smoothing	167
Spirit Varnishing	168
French Polishing, Situations, Rubbers	171
Rags, Wettings, Rubbings	172
Directions for Repolishing	174
General Remarks and Useful Receipts	175

INTRODUCTION.

THE very great improvement which the arts and manufactures of this country have attained, within the last fifty years, renders it essential that every person engaged therein should use his utmost endeavours to obtain a perfect knowledge of the trade or art which he professes to follow. The workmen of the last century were, comparatively speaking, with but few exceptions, mechanical beings, who worked by rule, unguided by any scientific principles, and followed step by step the beaten track of their ancestors. The workmen of the present day have the road of science opened for them;

the clue of knowledge is unwound to the inquiring mind ; but unless industry and perseverance accompany them in the pursuit of information, they will never obtain sufficient to justify a pretension even to a medium knowledge of the principles of their respective arts.

These remarks apply to scientific and mechanical professions generally ; but to the cabinet-maker and upholsterer they attach with peculiar force. It is not enough for a person following either of these branches of domestic decoration to have attained the character of a *good workman*, that being now considered a mere negative phrase, implying only that quantum of excellence which consists in following implicitly the directions of others, or imitating with neatness and accuracy their details and plans. In a business where change and caprice rule with unbounded sway, in which the fashion of to-day may become obsolete to-morrow, and in which novelty forms the greatest recommendation—an inventive genius and a discriminating judgment are, certainly, essential qualifications; and if the young workman ever feels the least ambition to excel, or entertains a wish to rise above the bench, he will find them to be not only essential, but actually indispensable.

In this business, as well as in many others, the workman who understands the principles of his trade. and applies them correctly in practice, has a decided advantage over his fellow-workmen ; and if to his superior knowledge he add a steadiness of manner and industrious habits, his endeavours cannot fail to secure approbation, while his worth will be certainly and duly appreciated.

If, then, in order to secure constant employment—the only means of insuring comfort to himself and family—it is essential that the *workman* should excel, how much more must it behoove the person who *superintends* a business of the kind to be fully acquainted with every department of the business? for how can any one pretend to direct others who is himself in need of information? Nor is this all; it will often fall to his province to sketch out new designs, or to alter or improve those in present use. If his employer, or a respectable customer, should not approve of the fashion or ornamental embellishment of any new article of furniture submitted to their approbation, a superintendent would feel himself sadly at a loss, if he could neither sketch out the improvements or alterations which his own genius might suggest, nor imbody those pointed out by others.

Again; the researches of the chemist are daily adding to a stock of information valuable to every department of the arts and sciences. Among these, the cabinet-maker and upholsterer will find many peculiarly serviceable—witness the modern improvements in cements, varnishes, gilding, polishing, and every other part of ornamental decoration. The experience of few, indeed, is sufficiently extensive to enable them to store their minds with one-tenth part of the information which has been published to the world on these heads. A work, therefore, which contains the most approved receipts, and from which the workman will be enabled to select those applicable to his purpose, will be appreciated as equally useful and necessary.

This work, a fifth time submitted to the public under the title of "The Cabinet-maker and Upholsterer's Companion," is intended as a book of useful information to the apprentice, a work of real utility to the workman, and a manual of experimental reference to the trade generally. It does not profess to give diffuse instructions how to make a table, a chair, or any similar article of furniture: that would be not only superfluous and unnecessary, but a vain attempt. Practice only—and that under good instruction—can make a good workman or a neat finisher. Our aim has been to produce a work which shall give those instructions which are not always to be met with in every one's practice, but which are not the less essential to be known by every workman.

To make our work useful, and easy of reference, we have adopted the popular plan of dividing the subjects into distinct parts, and of again subdividing them under their proper heads. This will enable any one to trace out any particular direction or receipt with facility, and show, generally at one view, all we have to say upon the subject.

Part I. comprises the rudiments and principles of ornamental cabinet-making and upholstery generally; and contains plain and familiar instructions, exemplified by easy examples, for attaining a proficiency in the art of drawing, particularly that department applicable to the cabinet-maker and upholsterer. In this part we have endeavoured to lead the student, step by step, from first principles to the more determinate forms; and, by placing before his view the progressive examples, to render the attainment of this useful art equally speedy and certain.

We have not only endeavoured, in this part, to practise the pupil in such a familiar and progressive manner as to render it a pleasing recreation, rather than an abstract study; but we have also laid down the most approved principles for the development and exercise of his inventive faculties, in the practice of the ornamental department of his art, and to lay before him such elegant and classic designs, and such modern examples of furniture, as will lead him instinctively to form a style at once chaste and appropriate.

Part II. comprises the processes of veneering, inlaying, and finishing in buhl-work the ornamental decorations used in cabinet-work. In this part, such directions are given as experience has warranted to be most certain of properly and successfully performing the embellishment in a neat and complete manner. The materials best adapted for the purpose are also pointed out, and the cements and glues most suited for this kind of work described.

Part III. comprises dyeing and staining woods, ivory, bone, tortoise-shell, musical instruments, and all other manufactured articles; with the processes of silvering, gilding, and bronzing. In this, we have laid down the most approved directions for the selection of the wood or other articles best adapted for the required process; the method of preparing it, and the dye or stain best calculated to give it the desired colour; and in the silvering, gilding, and bronzing, nothing has been omitted which modern improvement has added to perfect in these branches the highest style of brilliancy.

Part IV. comprises lackering, japanning, varnishing, and polishing every article of cabinet and upholstery work; and contains all the improved processes practised in each of their departments, including India japanning and the French polishing; together with plain directions for making and employing the best and most brilliant lackers, japans, and varnishes, according to the receipts of the most celebrated manufacturers.

Part V. contains glues, cement, and compositions for filling up and ornamenting articles of furniture; and a considerable number of miscellaneous receipts—the result of experience, or selected from the writings of the most approved authors and the more scientific works.

Such is the outline of its contents. As to its merits, we submit our opinion to the test of a discerning public, in the confident expectation that the "Cabinet-maker and Upholsterer's Companion" will soon find a place in every factory and workshop, and be the companion of every intelligent workman.

THE
CABINET-MAKER
AND
UPHOLSTERER'S COMPANION.

PART I.
Ornamental Cabinet-Making.

THE RUDIMENTS OF DRAWING, AS APPLICABLE TO ARTICLES OF FURNITURE—PRIMARY OBSERVATIONS ON DRAWING ORNAMENTS FOR CABINET-WORK—GEOMETRICAL AND PERSPECTIVE TERMS DEFINED AND EXPLAINED—THE RUDIMENTS OF SHADOWING AND OF COLOURING—ORNAMENTS USED IN CABINET-WORK; THEIR TERMS EXPLAINED — ORNAMENTAL DECORATIONS; WHERE AND WHEN MOST APPLICABLE.

THE RUDIMENTS OF DRAWING,
AS APPLICABLE TO ARTICLES OF FURNITURE.

DRAWING is the art of delineating on an appropriate surface the representations of subjects as they appear to the eye or are formed by the inventive powers of a correct taste. It takes in a wide range, but the parts more intimately connected with cabinet-work are—Geometry and Perspective.

Geometrical drawing may be defined to be that branch which delineates any given object according to certain fixed forms or proportions, and represents the whole subject apportioned by a given scale. Perspective, on the contrary, represents it in the same manner as the eye actually beholds the given figure, the fore parts being most conspicuous, while those distant appear more indistinct, or rather as if they receded from the sight.

The preparatory studies consist in various modes of delineating the outline by light and dark strokes; the more mature operations of the art are—shadowing and colouring.

Drawing of this description may be divided into outline and shading; the outline, or contour, represents the boundaries of an object, as they appear to terminate against the background, and is a section of the whole mass. Outlines are also used for the circumscription of all the parts of an object, interior as well as exterior; while shading, with a softer pencil, expresses the projections, cavities, or flatness which form its anterior features.

A correct outline of the objects of a picture is of the highest importance, and certainly the best test of an intelligent draughtsman; as, in most cases, it conveys the general character of the object without the aid of shading, and is therefore, as far as it goes, a complete drawing in itself. The aim of the student, therefore, should be to acquire the power of copying faithfully whatever may present itself before him.

For the first essay, no material is better than a soft pencil; the drawing to be sketched on white paper, and the pencil to be held somewhat in the same manner as a pen, but so as to allow of more freedom of action, and to give a greater facility of motion both to the fingers and the wrist. The learner should begin with making lines parallel, straight, and curved in all directions, and then exercise himself in tracing geometrical figures, into some of which all forms may be resolved; but without, as yet, the aid of either rule or compass. He should also copy occasionally from broad specimens of ornament, as being well adapted to give firmness and flexibility to the hand; to increase which they should be practised upon as large a scale as convenient. He may also, at intervals, study from the best drawings, or from open chalk prints.

Whatever be the object to be drawn, its general form should be first sketched out very slightly, that any fault may be the more easily removed. Estimate, as nearly as you can, the distances of particular points in the original figure; make dots at similar distances on your paper; then draw your lines carefully to those dots, beginning at the upper part, and working downward, either from right to left, or from left to right, according to the tendency of the parts. Draw the principal divisions first; when these appear right, mark in the smaller parts, and when the whole is pencilled out, examine it scrupulously; then pass over it with a piece of bread, to render the lines nearly invisible, and revise and retouch them again and again, till the sketch be correct. After this, go over the whole with a harder pencil; or the lines may be put in ink with a sable brush, first comparing all the parts with the original, both perpendicularly and horizontally, that they may have the same comparative inclination, range, and distance as the object itself. Where the student is at a loss, he may now sparingly use the compass or sector, but only by way of proving the angles

after he has done his utmost, for unless these in
struments be more used in the eye than in the hand
of the learner, he will never make a good draughtsman, or be able to judge of distance in any other
way than by rule. Perhaps it would be best for
learners to make their first lessons as near the size
of the originals as possible; and, when the eye
can measure with tolerable exactness, to vary from
these dimensions will be proper; the pupil will
then acquire an aptness of preserving similar proportions on a different scale, which forms so essential a part of the draughtsman's skill, and is so
indispensable in imitating objects or drawings. It
is not necessary that the lines in a drawing should
be of one uniform thickness; on the contrary, a
delicate variety, with the lines occasionally broken,
gives a richness, and adds much to the effect. The
lines may also be carried a little within the contour
of the hollows, as if pursuing the inflection on the
part, which, when done with skill, makes a mere
outline very characteristic.

These remarks apply to drawing generally; we
shall now give a few primary observations regard
ing the principles of the art, as applied to cabinet
and upholstery work.

PRIMARY OBSERVATIONS

ON DRAWING ORNAMENTS

FOR CABINET-WORK.

It will be to little purpose that the young workman should possess a correct discrimination in the choice of the most appropriate ornaments, if he have not some knowledge of drawing; for without he can delineate the embellishment in outline, he will never be enabled to execute it in wood. For this purpose, his first acquirement must be to trace an object by the eye, in all its relative proportions and inclinations, with a just boldness and freedom of hand. To facilitate this, his best way will be to begin by drawing the most simple forms, as straight lines, and proceed gradually to the more complex objects; but whatever subject be his first essay, he must place it perpendicularly and directly before him, otherwise he will never produce a correct drawing. He must also bear in mind, while he is copying, what are the details of the object, as well as what is merely before him; otherwise he will never learn to delineate with correctness

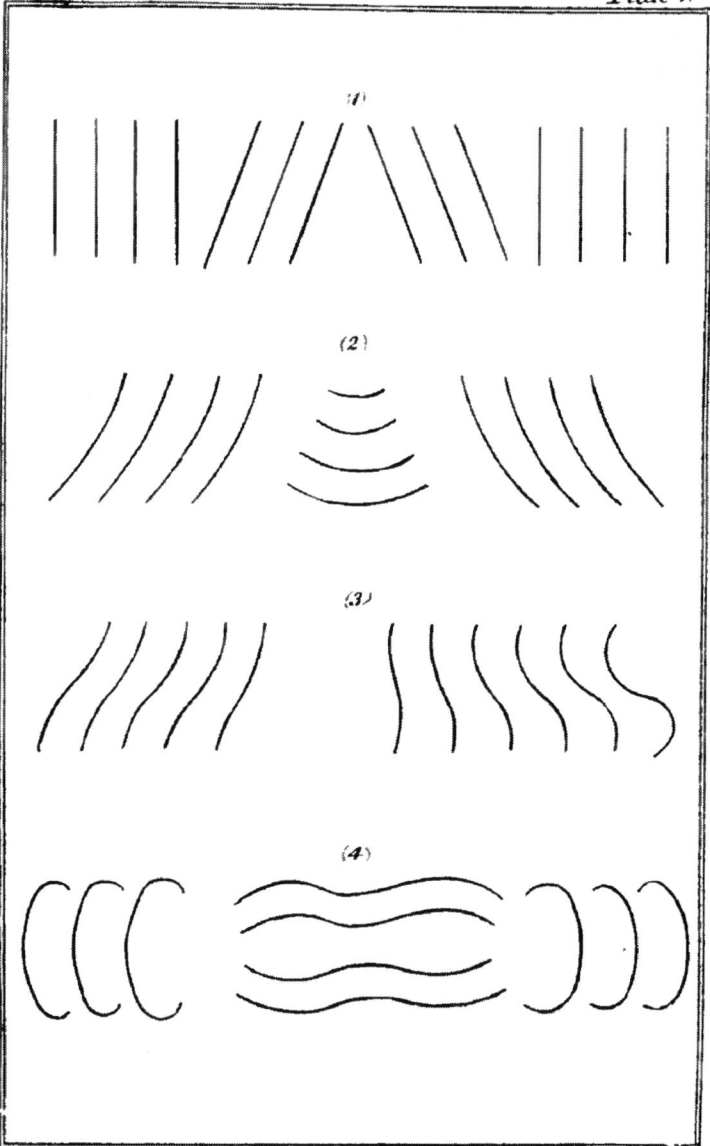

Simple Lines & Forms.

Lesson II

Plate 2

Simple & Compound Lines & Forms.

From straight lines, he should next proceed to curved and spiral ones of different descriptions, branching off to the right hand and to the left. In this he must be particular, although he will at first find it somewhat difficult to make his sides correspond.

After drawing lines in all the various directions his fancy can dictate, he will acquire a command of hand, and a ready facility of delineating in every possible position.

The best method of learning, generally, is for the pupil to draw a few simple parallel lines, and after this to copy curved lines, and then to multiply them to the number of ten or more; these being done, he may try leaves and scrolls; and lastly, the whole ramifications of foliage.

We will illustrate this part of our introductory instruction with several lessons, by way of examples.—*See Plates* 2 *and* 3.

Plate 2, *Lesson* 1. Various simple lines, for the pupil's first practice.

Plate 3, *Lesson* 2. Simple and compound lines and forms, with a figure (10) in outline, half shade and full shade.

These preliminary lessons should be well practised

before the pupil proceeds further onwards; for, however simple they may seem, they are as necessary and important a part of drawing as the foundation-stone is to the building: they are, indeed, the very laws of the art; and it is by a tasteful combination of these forms, that the most correct pictures and the most accurate delineations are produced.

Having practised thus far, the student may next attempt the combinations, or compound forms,— as terminal ornaments, vases, pedestals, columns, leaves, scrolls, and similar embellishments. Of these we shall give a few lessons, but which, in the hand of a judicious student, will be amply sufficient.—*See Plates* 4 *and* 5.

Plate 4, *Lesson* 3. Various compound ornaments and scrolls, in outline and shade, peculiarly suitable for cabinet-work, and well adapted as practical lessons to the pupil.

Plate 5, *Lesson* 4. Compound ornaments continued.

When the student has copied these over several times, and attained sufficient practice in copying from drawings with precision, and can measure distances with the eye, and delineate them with a free hand, he should then try at drawing from

Lesson III. Plate 3.

Compound Ornaments in line & Shade

Lesson IV. Plate 4.

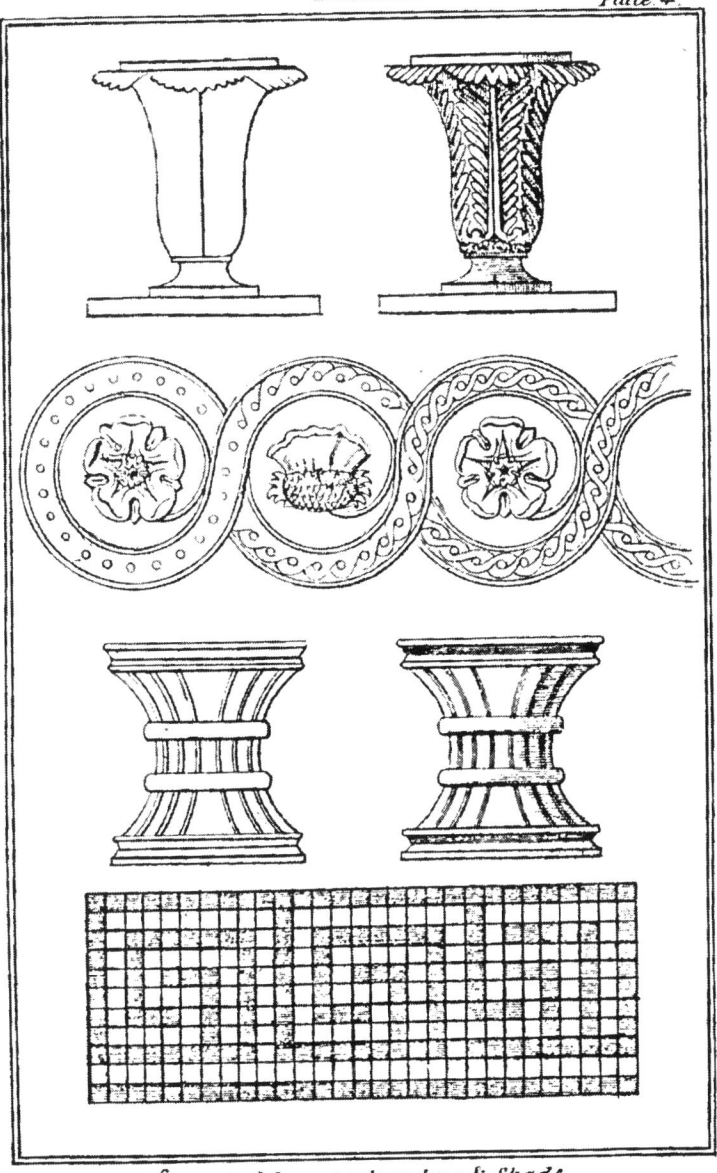

Compound Ornaments in line & Shade

plaster-casts; after which he may practise from the vegetable creation such plants and flowers as are best calculated for his future purpose. By proceeding thus, he will soon become proficient; he may therefore now try the fertility of his own powers, by applying himself to the composing of ornaments, which will rarely fail to appear graceful, rich, and natural.

In designing ornaments, the pupil must picture the whole subject in his imagination, as though drawn on the paper before him; he should then, with a black-lead pencil, mark it out faintly in lightly-sketched lines, which, having completed, he may lower the whole with crumbs of bread, and lastly, retrace it more correctly. The ornament may now be inked with a pen, or with a fine sable-hair brush, or worked up in pencil, as the artist may consider best.

GEOMETRICAL AND PERSPECTIVE TERMS
DEFINED AND EXPLAINED.

WE have said that the parts of drawing more intimately connected with our subject, are Geometry and Perspective. It will therefore be necessary that the terms in common use be defined, as, without a knowledge of them, it will be almost impossible to understand many of the directions essential to the cabinet-maker or upholsterer.

GEOMETRY.

Extension is a term applied to any expanded surface, proceeding in any or every direction.

Magnitude is a solid bulk, having length, breadth, and thickness.

A *figure* is any bounded space. When formed of a plain surface, it is termed a *plain* figure.

A *superficial* figure has length and breadth only.

A *solid* figure has length, breadth, and thickness.

Surfaces are the extremities of solids.

Lines are the confines of *surfaces*.

Points are the terminations or intersections of lines.

Angles are the concentration or conjunction of two inclined lines, and are either right, acute, or obtuse.

A *curve* is that kind of line from which, if two points be taken, the intersected point is not straight.

A *quadrangle* is a plain, square figure, bounded by four right lines.

A *parallelogram* is an oblong quadrangle, the opposite sides of which are perfectly parallel.

A *quadrilateral* is a quadrangle formed by four equal lines.

A *rhombus* is a quadrangle, having its sides equal, and its angles two equally obtuse, and two equally acute.

A *rhomboid* is an oblique-angled parallelogram, whose opposite sides and angles are equal to each other.

A *trapezium* is a figure with none of its sides parallel.

A *trapezoid* hath two, only, of its opposite sides parallel.

All plain figures, having more than four sides, are termed *polygons*, and are named from the number of sides they contain: five sides, a *pentagon;* six, a *hexagon;* seven, a *heptagon;* eight, an *octagon*, &c.

A *circle* is formed by a uniform curved line, called its *circumference*, which curve is in every part equally distant from the point termed its *centre*.

A *triangle* is a figure having three sides.

A *semicircle* is half a circle.

A *segment of a circle* is more or less than half of circle.

The *diameter of a circle* is a straight line drawn

through the centre, each end joining to the circumference.

A *chord* is a right line drawn within a circle, its ends both joining the extremities of the arc.

The *radius of a circle* is a right line drawn from the centre to the circumference.

The construction or formation of most of these geometrical figures or parts are so self-evident, from their definition, that we need not give any delineation of their figure, but leave them for the student's exercise; in which, indeed, he can scarcely fail of correctness. We shall therefore now proceed to

PERSPECTIVE.

If the student hold up, at arm's-length, a picture-frame in which is a square or oblong piece of glass washed over with whitehard varnish, but perfectly dry, he will be enabled to delineate with a pencil the visible lineaments or outline appearance of the object as seen within the compass of the frame; which result will be the lineal picture, the glass being considered the paper on which the object is to be drawn. The true relative proportions of perspective will be here laid down; and if, after the design is sketched out, the whole is proportioned by a scale, it will greatly facilitate the student, particularly if he should afterward wish to enlarge or decrease the size of his object. In this case, a border may be drawn at equal or certain distances from the extremities of every part; and the whole space, both in breadth and depth, be apportioned into equal divisions, and marked by pencil lines intersecting the whole and each other; and if on a larger or smaller paper, the same number of divisions be made, the student will have a guide which will hardly allow him to err in preserving the due and relative proportions in the copy as existed in the original. To illustrate this, see *plate* 1, *diag.* 1. The spectator is viewing the appearance which two pieces of furniture will have at a distance; when seen through a similar medium to the one just named, the result will be the same, and prove this position in perspective to be correct, viz. that all subjects situated on a level floor, diminish, and seem to advance up or ascend the picture, in the same proportion as they recede from the sight, while these suspended from or on a level ceiling, have the appearance of *descending*, or seeming lower in the picture, in the same proportion, according to their distance from the eye of the spectator.

Diagram 2 will show the terms made use of, for example, the figure represents a hall which is thrown into perspective; in this case A B are the base lines, C D the points of view, or distance: the line which is drawn from the one to the other is the horizontal line, and E is the point of sight. We have divided the base line into six equal parts, to show the dimension of each square (for we will suppose the hall to be paved); from each of these divisions draw lines to the point of sight, E: then draw diagonal lines from the extremities of your base line to the points of view, and where the visual lines are cut by the diagonal ones, draw parallel lines, and the diminution of each square will be given correctly. It will be easily seen we have determined the width of the door at two squares on the base, which, carried to the point of distance, intersect the side wall, and give the width against it; the thickness is likewise carried out on the base line, and carried to the points of sight E, and gives the depth of the door. Thus, by practising a few similar plans, the first rudiments of the art will be easily understood, and found both useful and amusing.

The following are the most common, and at the same time the most essential, terms used in perspective.

The *point of view* is the optic angle of the visual rays, or point where the rays from the picture or object concentrate; and where the spectator is supposed to stand while drawing the object—it is consequently out of the picture, but is the point or distance from which only will the picture or object appear natural.

The *point of sight*, or more properly the *seat of the eye*, is a point in the picture directly opposite the eye, and is produced by a line drawn at right angles to the picture.

The *horizontal line* is a line passing before, and of the exact height of the eye of the spectator.

The *primitive object* is the figure given to be delineated.

Primitive measures are the real measures of the object reduced to a scale, which by being thrown obliquely into perspective, will be seen foreshortened.

The *base plane* is the floor or part on which the object is supposed to be situated.

The *base line*, or entering line, is that on which the transparent plane is supposed to be placed.

The *vanishing points* are those in the horizontal line to which all the oblique points concentrate or meet.

Inclined vanishing points are ascertained by perpendicular lines raised from the extreme vanishing point in the horizontal line; and are essential for pediments and swing-glasses.

The *diagonal vanishing point* is a point set off upon the horizontal line either way from the *seat of the eye;* and in the same proportionate measure as the draughtsman is supposed to stand distant from the picture, or object.

THE RUDIMENTS OF SHADOWING.

When the objects are correctly drawn in outline, the learner should proceed with shadowing, first laying on the dark broad washes, then the next in strength, and lastly the more delicate half-tints. In finishing, great attention must be paid to the quantities and combinations of light, middle tint, shadow, and reflection : in this, the young student will find some difficulty in distinguishing the delicate gradations of light and shade; but observation and practice will soon teach him. We may, however, remark, that he must reserve his greatest strength of light and shade for the parts most prominent, and every light must be accompanied and supported by its shade; the middle tint becomes deeper in tone as it advances from the light, till it is lost in the shadow, and the outline is softened into the background, by reflections from the surrounding objects; the contour, therefore, must not be too strongly marked; or the extreme parts, which should retire, will come forward.

Shadows are made out by washing or tinting the drawing with India ink, which should never be mixed up for use a second time, after having once dried in the saucer, or it will work muddy. A neutral tint, made with Venetian red and indigo, or lamp-black, burnt terra de sienna, and lake, varied as circumstances and distance may require, may also be used for this purpose.

Shading may be performed on columns or other convex bodies in two different ways: the first is, that of laying on the shades, as nearly in their places as possible, with a tint very nearly dark enough, then softening off the edges with a clean brush with water, and, when dry, repeating the process several times, until sufficiently lightened: the other is, by working with tints rather lighter than are requisite, at first laid in spots near each other, and then blended by a faint wash over the whole, and when nearly dry, strengthen by other spots in the interstices, and so on, gradually giving the shades their due force and form, leaving the paper for the lights. This mode is called *stippling*, and in the hands of a master, is the best, or at least the boldest, for finished drawings; for it not only occasions the whole picture to sparkle, but gives a transparency and play to the shadows, making, as it were, darkness visible. It is, however, of little importance which of these, or any other plan of shading, be adopted, so that the faithfulness of the imitation be well attended to.

In the representations of shadows, the artist should be careful not to make them too hard or abrupt at the edges, because every shadow terminates by the faint and indistinct transition from the obscure to the illuminated part of the surface upon which such shadows are cast. Nor should shadows be equally dark; for it is to be remembered that shadows projected by the sun are softened by the surrounding rays and by the general diffusion of light through the atmosphere: they should, therefore, be darkest near the object that produces them. It is on this principle that shadows from the light of a candle are darker than those of the sun; although the light is much more forcible from the latter body: hence it follows, that shadows in candlelight scenes must, in the language of painting, be heavier in their representation, or less transparent than those of daylight.

For examples of shadowing, see fig. 10, plate 3, and plates 4 and 5.

THE RUDIMENTS OF COLOURING.

A JUDICIOUS writer has observed, that "should the most skilful master draw a rose or grape with the pencil only, his observers would have but a faint or imperfect image of the object; but let him add to each its proper colours, and we no longer doubt—we smell the rose, we touch the grape." Colouring may, therefore, be considered as the life and soul of a picture: it is the third and last component—that of giving to objects their proper hue and colour, as they appear under all the combinations of light, middle tint, and shadow; and also of blending and contrasting them, so as to make each appear with the greatest brilliancy and advantage.

Colouring may be divided into two kinds: that which is necessary for rendering the imitation just and natural; and that which is fascinating, and renders the work more impressive on the imagination, more delightful to the eye. Truth alone, in the local tints, is required in the first; the second demands choice in their selection, for the eye has the same intuitive abhorrence of inharmonious combinations of colour, that the ear has to discordant sounds. To possess a scientific knowledge of the arrangement of colours, so as to produce effects not unnatural, requires but little talent; but to perform all that a skilful combination and application of the various powers of colours can effect, is not so easily attained.

As, however, the student may by this time have attained a sufficient knowledge of drawing to be able to portray any object he sees, his fancy may invent, or his employer suggest, he will now only require a few hints as to the colours that may be compounded with the best effect for imitating, in drawings, the different woods, metals, cloths, &c., used in the various articles of cabinet-furniture, stating the principal colours first.

To imitate mahogany.—Mix light red with burnt umber; shadow with burnt umber.

Rosewood.—Mix lake and lampblack; shadow with a stronger tint of the same while wet.

Satin-wood.—Use yellow ochre; shadow with Vandyke brown.

Bronze.—Mix Prussian blue, gamboge, and burnt umber; shadow with Vandyke brown and indigo, mixed.

Brass.—Use gamboge; shadow with burnt terra de sienna, and stipple with burnt umber. *Inlaid brass* or *buhl ornaments* may be laid on afterwards with a body-colour made of gamboge and whiting.

Ormolu.—Mix king's yellow and Indian yellow.

Velvet.—Mix carmine and Indian red.

Green-baize.—Mix indigo and gamboge. For chair-seats, use vermilion.

Glass.—Mix lampblack and indigo; shadow with the same.

Porphyry marble.—Mix lake, Venetian red, and ivory-black; afterward speckle with constant-white and with lampblack.

Verd-antique.—Mix indigo and Roman ochre; afterward lay on light and dark-green spots.

Sienna marble.—Mix raw terra de sienna and burnt umber; vein it with burnt umber alone.

Mona marble.—Mix indigo, Venetian red, and lake; vein with dark green.

Black marble.—Mix indigo and madder-brown with lampblack.

Buff-colour drapery.—Mix gamboge and Roman ochre, or gamboge and a little lake; shadow with the same, darker. For the more intense shadows, mix gamboge and burnt umber.

White drapery.—Shade with a mixture of India ink and indigo.

Chintz.—Shadow with a mixture of lake and gamboge.

Crimson curtains.—Colour with red lead and a little lake.

Gilt poles.—Colour as for *ormolu,* and shadow with burnt umber and gamboge combined, or with burnt umber and lake, and sometimes with a mixture of lake and gamboge.

There is scarcely an artist but who compounds colours each in a manner peculiar to himself. Now, as landscapes are sometimes seen through the apertures of windows, when a view of the room is taken, some instruction is necessary in this department of the art. We shall, therefore, state what is considered to be the best and simplest process.

After the view is pencilled out, begin the *sky;* for this, use a mixture of Prussian blue and a little lake; begin at the top of the picture, and soften it downwards, but at the horizon add a little Venetian red. The *clouds* are next to be worked in, with a mixture of Venetian red, indigo, and a little gamboge; next, with the sky-colour and a little Venetian red added, cover the whole of the *ground*, beginning at the front, and thinning it towards the horizon; but observe not to go over the *rivers*, or pieces of *water*. *Distant mountains* are coloured with indigo and lake; *near, fuscus mountains*, with indigo, lake, and burnt terra de sienna; *distant parts of the grass* are made with indigo, yellow-ochre, and lake; *near grass* is made with burnt sienna, Italian pink, and indigo; *dark touches* on the *foreground* are of Vandyke brown, indigo, and burnt terra de sienna; *intense dark touches*, of lampblack and burnt umber; *distant trees* are worked with indigo, lake, and gamboge, shadowed with the same colour, made darker; and *near trees* are coloured with burnt sienna, gamboge, and indigo, deepened towards the shadowed side. This is all that is required to be known in this branch of the art; and is a complete and valuable, though concise, process for painting cabinet-furniture, landscapes, &c.

ORNAMENTS USED IN CABINET-WORK

THEIR TERMS EXPLAINED.

ORNAMENTS are the decorative parts of an edifice, household furniture, or other objects, studied from the vegetable and animal kingdoms, gracefully and artificially combined. They are seldom of importance on the exteriors of buildings—simplicity and variety in the contour, with bold, massive forms, being there primarily considered, and on which their grandeur chiefly depends. It is in the interior that ornaments should be principally applied, when they are not liable to be destroyed by the weather, and are likewise brought nearer to the eye of the beholder.

Foliage ornament is composed of leaves only; the subdivisions of a leaf are called *raffles*, and the small, external divisions, *plants;* the terminations of the plants are called *eyes*, and the longer reeds, proceeding from the eyes, are called *pipes*. The leaves chiefly used are the acanthus, olive, palm, parsley, vine, ivy, oak, thistle, laurel, lotus, and water-leaf; the flowers most in use are the honey-suckle, lotus, lily, rose, and jasmine.

Mixed ornament is a composition of leaves, fruit,

flowers, and scrolls, combined in any way with each other.

Festooned ornament is comprised of fruit, flowers, and leaves, intermixed with each other, and supported at the two extremities with ribbons, sometimes suspended from a bull's horns, the middle part formed into a parabolic curve by its gravity.

Arabesque ornament is a mixture of slender scrolls, leaves, vases, birds, lyres, and representations of human figures.

Winding foliage has a principal plant from which issues a stem in the form of a serpentine line, with a number of branches spreading out on each side of all the convex parts of the alternate sides, and twisting themselves in the form of spiral lines; and those spirals and stalks are decorated with foliage and flowerets.

Serpentined, or running ornament has a trunk, from which springs a stem continually changing its course in opposite directions, that is, first concave, then convex, and so on alternately to any multipled number of curves of contrary natures, from the concave and convex parts shoot branches, each terminating with a rose.

Plaited ornament is a definite number of serpentine lines, interwoven with each other; and exclusively in the cap of the Grecian Ionic order.

Guilloche ornament is a succession of circles entwining each other.

Fret ornament is formed of straight lines like the wards of a key; used much by the Etruscans on their vases.

Mosaic ornament is a cemented inlay of marbles, glass, shells, and rich varied stones; used in pavements, and on tops of tables.

Buhl ornament is an insertion of brass, and sometimes of wood, formed into foliages, flowers, animals, &c.

ORNAMENTS USED IN CABINET AND UPHOLSTERY WORK:

WHEN AND WHERE MOST APPLICABLE.

The ornamental, or decorative parts of furniture should be cautiously introduced; and when applied, should be designed with regularity and distinctness of outline; they should also be of a character simple, and appropriate to the work of which they are intended to form the embellishment.

You may lay it down as a general rule, that

when a corresponding ornament cannot readily be adopted, one of an opposite character is not admissible ; and in that case, an ornament of no peculiar character is the only alternative.

In addition to the essential modifications of utility and convenience, the secondary objects, elegance and beauty, are indispensably necessary to be studied, to render each piece of furniture what it should certainly be—a graceful, pleasing, and appropriate article.

Hall chairs.—The family arms, or crest, carved tastefully, and emblazoned in their proper colours, form a most appropriate embellishment.

Library chairs.—Classic ornaments, such as the wreath of laurel, two genii striving for the bays, Minerva's bird, or others of a similar character, may be introduced with good effect.

Drawing-room chairs admit of an infinity of embellishment : Apollo's lyre, the Graces, tastefully devised scrolls, flowers, wreaths, and others of an appropriate description, may be executed either in buhl-work or in carved relief, as most suited to the character of the ornament chosen.

Card-tables, being used for breakfast purposes, as well as for the evening party, may have the tea or coffee-plant for their ornaments, or the masks of Ceres, Bacchus, or Comus; but for a dining table, the cornucopia, or some bold or chaste design of fruit, is decidedly the more appropriate. Stars and flowers have been introduced into this part of cabinet furniture; but a greater perversion of taste can be scarcely conceived.

Library and writing tables should be embellished altogether from mythological history: the head of Mercury, placed on partitions between the drawers, is very appropriate, this god being said to be the inventor of letters; the caduceus is also well adapted for an ornament; so is the papyrus-plant, from which paper was first made; the laurel-wreath, or the bays, may likewise be used; but no other trees, flower, or shrub should on any account be introduced unless, indeed, we except the oak, ink being made from the galls produced by this tree. Besides Mercury, Apollo, the god of poetry, Cadmus, the inventor of part of the alphabet, and Clio, the presiding muse of history, are all appropriate embellishments, if applied with effect and in good taste.

Dining tables.—Broad ornaments are most consistent; the bread-tree and its fruit form an admirable subject; hops also, though a simple plant, form a very beautiful ornament when chased and inserted in wood. The mask of Ceres, with the corn in her hair, is also well suited to the dining-room.

Drawing-room tables may be properly embellished with any tastefully designed ornament of fruit or flowers.

Sofas require, like the rest of the furniture, that their ornaments should be appropriate, chaste, and tasteful: the couch-flower, the heart's-ease, honeysuckles, eglantines, or Turkish ornaments nay be used with good effect; a greyhound couchant may adorn the end of the sofa.

Ottomans should be ornamented with the lyre, or with musical instruments, or wreaths. Commodes are sometimes placed at each end of ottomans; the panels of which may be embellished with a winged figure of Victory, and the pedestals surmounted by two antique urns.

A dressing table, or toilette, may be embellished with subjects chosen either from Mythology or Botany; the Graces, or foliage and flowers of scent-producing plants.

Window-seats in Drawing-rooms.—The Egyptian lotus or water-lily, or any flower characteristic of rest and composure, may be very properly carved in wood, or inserted in buhl. English heart's-ease, and peony flowers, are of this cast. The mouldings, too, should be optically studied, that their whole contour may be visible below the eye, as well as where even with the horizon.

For cheval dressing glasses, the lotus, or waterlily, is admirably adapted; or the figure of Narcissus, viewing his own image in the water, would be very appropriate. For a pier commode and glass, chimeras, consoles, or turned pillars, are well suited. A laurel-wreath contended for by two genii, or the bust of Pallas, or Pluto, may be very consistently chosen for ladies' bookcases, with cabinet attached.

Sideboards may be adorned with the mask of Bacchus, or the horn of plenty; and on the backboard the thyrsus, or sceptre of Bacchus, will form a very beautiful ornament; the cellaret may have vine-leaves and clustered leaves, serpentined and festooned. Bacchanalian youths gathering grapes, if tastefully finished, would be an admirable ornament for this article of furniture.

The cot-bed admits a great variety of ornament. The head of Nox, the goddess of night; the stars, as her attendants; and a bunch of pop pies, as producing sleep, may be all introduced with good effect; guardian genii or angels, doves, and many similar emblems, may be occasionally applied. White drapery, as emblematical of infantile purity, is at all times most proper.

Bedsteads may be appropriately adorned with wreaths of nightshade, stars, a mask of Somnus, the starry hyacinth, the great Arabian star-flower, the poppy, or any other nocturnal plant or flower.

For drawing-room window-drapery, the embellishments to be chosen should be pine-apples, pomegranates, artichokes, or melons. The drapery and testers, for drawing-rooms, should have flowers only, such as the passion-flower, the star of Bethlehem, or the rhododendron. The sun-flower looks well, but is rather common, and therefore unfit to be introduced into elegant apartments.

Libraries should be finished in imitation of the antique: the embellishments should be of a strictly classical description. The owl and olive-branch, the laurel, Pegasus, the Olympic games in relief, are very appropriate; or the twelve signs of the zodiac may be inlaid with mosaic work.

Fire-screens have a number of analogous ornaments: Jove's thunderbolt, the phœnix rising out of flames, the cyclops, Vesta, the goddess of fire, or a representation of the fall of Phæton. These ornaments are equally appropriate for grates; as are also serpents vomiting forth fire. Fish or swans are applicable to a basin-stand; and an eagle to support a chandelier.

The preceding are some of the most tasteful and appropriate designs for the various articles of furniture described; and are intended to give the young cabinet-maker an insight into that most essential part of his business—the properly finishing and embellishing his work with *appropriate* ornaments only—a desideratum overlooked by too many workmen of the present day, some of whom, it would appear, seem more desirous to load their work with ornament than to study its fitness or appropriateness to the article in hand. A correct taste, a bold design, and a careful application, will insure to a workman not only the respect of his employers, but will necessarily entail constant employ and liberal remuneration.

PART II.

Veneering, Inlaying, etc.

OF VENEERING, INLAYING, AND EXECUTING IN BUHL-WORK THE ORNAMENTAL PART OF CABINET AND UPHOLSTERY WORK.

VENEERING is the method of covering an inferior wood with a surface of a very superior kind, so that the parts of the article of furniture thus manufactured, which meet the eye, appear to the same advantage as if the whole work were of the best description. If this be well performed, it is very durable, looks well to the last, and is attainable at an expense considerably less than a similar article would cost if manufactured of the same wood throughout, but of an inferior quality.

The principal requisite to insure success in veneering, is to select well-seasoned wood for the ground, and to use the best and strongest glue. Be careful to exclude the air in gluing on your veneer, or a blister will arise, and spoil your work in that part. We need not add any more to these remarks, as the following process contains the most essential directions necessary in this department.

Gluing and veneering, as applicable to card and other table tops, secretary and bookcase fronts, &c.

It is a desideratum among workmen to veneer their work in such a manner that it will stand. Several of the methods commonly used cause the piece either to warp in winding, or otherwise to get hollow, after the work is finished, on its upper side; and however careful the workman may be in laying his veneer, this will sometimes happen. Much depends upon the manner of preparing the ground, perhaps more than in that of laying the veneer. Select that piece of deal which is freest from knots; slit it down the middle, or, take a piece out of the heart, and place the boards, when cut to the required length, in a warm place for two or three days; then joint them up, placing a heart edge and an outside edge together; when dry, cut your top again between each joint, and joint it afresh; you will then have a top glued up of pieces about two inches wide, and if you have been careful in making your joints good, you will have a top not so liable to cast, after it is veneered, as many of the tops which are now done by the method usually in practice.

You may use wainscot or other wood, instead of deal, but make your joints in the same manner. It is also a good plan, after having veneered your top, to lay it on the ground with some shavings, with the veneer downwards; it then dries gradually, and is much less likely to cast than by drying too quick.

To raise old veneers.

In repairing old cabinets, and other furniture, workmen are sometimes at a loss to know how to get rid of those blisters which appear on the surface, in consequence of the glue under the veneer failing, or causing the veneer to separate from the ground in patches; and these blisters are frequently so situated, that without separating the whole veneer from the ground, it is impossible to introduce any glue between them, to relay it, the great difficulty, in this case, is to separate the veneer from the ground without injuring it, as it adheres, in many places, too fast to separate without breaking it. We will here, therefore, show how this operation may be performed without difficulty, and the veneer preserved perfectly whole and uninjured, ready for relaying as a new piece. First, wash the surface with boiling water, and, with a coarse cloth, remove dirt or grease; then place it before the fire, or heat it with a caul; oil its surface with common linseed-oil, place it again to the fire, and the heat will make the oil penetrate quite through the veneer, and soften the glue underneath; then, whilst hot, raise the edge gently with a chisel, and it will separate completely from the ground: be careful not to use too great force, or you will spoil your work. Again, if it should get cold during the operation, apply more oil, and heat it again. Repeat this process till you have entirely separated the veneer, then wash off the old glue, and proceed to lay it again as a new veneer.

A strong glue, well suited for inlaying or veneering.

The best glue is readily known by its transparency, and being of a rather light brown, free from clouds and streaks. Dissolve this in water, and to every pint add half a gill of the best vinegar and half an ounce of isinglass.

To veneer tortoise-shell.

First, observe to have your shell of an equal thickness, and scrape and clean the under side very smooth; grind some vermilion very fine, and mix it up with spirits of turpentine and varnish; lay two or three coats of colour on the under side of the shell, till it becomes opaque; when dry, lay it down with good glue.

BUHL-WORK.

Buhl-work is the art of inlaying in brass, silver, ivory, tortoise-shell, &c., and if well executed has an admirable effect. It was introduced into this country some years since, and is now brought to a state of perfection which equals any thing of foreign manufacture. It is now in very general use, and although almost a distinct branch of itself, it is certainly an essential part of cabinet-work, and as such no workman should be entirely ignorant how to perform it.

Inlaying, as it is commonly termed, that is, with fancy woods, has been too long in use to require any particular directions. Buhl-work is nothing more than inlaying in metals, turtle or tortoise-shell, ivory, or the like; and the chief difficulty seems to be in the method of cutting out the pieces for inlaying, and of introducing them in a proper manner as a veneer or inlay to the work. Our directions for sketching and drawing ornaments will here be of great use, and a careful attention to the following directions will enable the persevering and ingenious workman to surmount every difficulty.

To prepare shell or brass ready for cutting out.

Being furnished with a thin piece of brass, of the thickness of the veneer, or as thin as can be conveniently worked, make the faces on both sides rough with a coarse file, or tooth-plane; take also a veneer of shell of the dimensions requisite, tooth that also; then warm your plates and veneers, pass a coat of glue first over a plate of brass; place over that a thin sheet of paper; glue that, and place your shell veneer on the top; place them between two smooth and even boards, either kept down by a heavy weight, or squeezed tight together by hand-screws; let them remain till dry, and they will adhere together sufficiently for the following purpose.

Cutting out the pattern.

Draw the pattern on your shell; if not sufficiently plain, paste a piece of paper on its surface, and let it dry, on which draw your design; being now provided with a bow-saw, the blade of which is very thin and narrow, such as may be made with a watch-spring, cut into about six strips, and the stretcher of the frame at a sufficient distance from the blade to enable you to turn in any direction, according to your pattern, and all made extremely light, begin by making a small hole in your veneer in a part where it will not so much be observed, (unless the pattern comes quite out to the edge,) and insert your saw; then very carefully follow the lines of your pattern till it is all cut through; you will then have two pieces, which may be separated by exposing them to steam or warm water; then take the two corresponding pieces, one of brass and one of shell, and when glued together according to the following direction, you will have two veneers, the counterparts in pattern with each other—only, where the brass is in one, the shell will be in the other.

To glue up the patterns.

Take two boards of sufficient dimensions, and heat them before the fire; rub them well with tallow to prevent the glue sticking to it; then take a sheet of paper, on which lay your veneer, and having well rubbed some strong glue into the vacancies where the pattern is to be inserted, put it carefully in its place, rubbing it down with a veneering-hammer, over which place another sheet of paper; place the whole between the hot boards, and press or screw them together with hand-screws; let them get quite dry—they will come out quite clean from the boards, and appear as one piece of veneer; you may then scrape the paper clean off—it is then ready for laying, or applying to your work.

Laying your veneer.

Having made your work perfectly level with a tooth-plane, apply to your veneer the glue recommended on page 48, and lay it on your work; then with a hot board, termed a caul, fasten it down by means of hand-screws, and let it remain till perfectly hard. It then only remains to be cleaned off and polished, according to the following directions.

In order to add to the beauty of your work, and produce a variety in the shade, it is necessary before laying your veneer to give that side intended to be glued a coat or two of some colour ground in oil, or varnish, and set by to dry thoroughly before you lay your veneer, as red lead and vermilion ground together; king's yellow, Prussian blue, or any colour you may fancy; and sometimes the surface is gilt on the side which you intend to lay on your work; this produces a very brilliant effect, and even the common Dutch metal applied will have a very good effect.

The method here given for tortoise-shell and brass is equally applicable to woods of two different colours, only then you need not use any other glue but that in common use, which must be good.

Inlaying with shaded wood.

Having shown the methods of cutting out and veneering, we need now only show the method used to produce that shady brown edge, on works inlaid with white holly, and which, when well executed, has a very pleasing and ornamental effect. The method is as follows:—

Into a shallow iron or tin pot, put a sufficient quantity of fine dry sand, to be level with the top edge of it; place it on the fire till it is quite hot; then, having your veneer cut out to the required pattern, dip the edges into the hot sand, and let them remain till the heat has made them quite brown; but be careful not to burn them. It is best to bring them to a proper colour by repeatedly renewing the operation than all at once, as you then do not injure the texture of the wood, and by immersing more or less of the edge, you produce a shaded appearance to your satisfaction. I would here recommend the workman, previous to beginning the operation, to have his pattern before him, shaded with umber, or any brown colour, in those parts that the wood is to be stained, as he then will be enabled, as he proceeds, to copy the various shades of the pattern, for the wood when once shaded cannot be altered; and as much of the beauty of this work depends on a proper judgment in placing your shadows, it is best always to have a guide to go by, that you may produce the best possible effect. Sometimes it is requisite to give a shadow in the centre, and not on the edge of your wood; and as this cannot be done by dipping it in the sand, you must do it by taking up a little of the hot sand, and sprinkling it, or heaping it up on those parts required to be darkened, letting it remain a short time, then shaking it off, and, if necessary, apply more where the colour is not deep enough.

To imitate inlaying of silver strings, &c.

This process is sometimes employed in the stocks, &c. of pistols, and if well executed has a very good effect The first thing is to determine as to your pattern, which you must carefully draw upon your work, and then engrave, or cut away the different lines with sharp gouges, chisels, &c., so as to appear clean and even,—taking care to cut them deep enough, and rather under, like a dovetail, to secure the composition afterwards to be put in the channels. The composition to resemble silver may be made as follows: Take any quantity of the purest and best grain-tin; melt it in a ladle or other convenient receptacle; add to it, while in fusion, the purest quicksilver, stirring it to make it incorporate; when you have added enough, it will remain in a stiff paste; if too soft, add more tin, and if not sufficiently fluid, add quicksilver; grind this composition on a marble slab, or in a mortar, with a little size, and fill up the cuttings or grooves in your work, as you would with a piece of putty; let it remain some hours to dry, when you may polish it off with the palm of your hand, and it will appear as if your work was inlaid with silver. Instead of tin, you may make a paste of silver-leaf and quicksilver, and proceed as above directed; you may also, for the sake of variety in your work, rub in wax of different colours, and having levelled the surface and cleaned off your work, hold it a moderate distance from the fire, which will give your strings a good gloss.

A glue for inlaying brass or silver strings, &c.

Melt your glue as usual, and to every pint add, of finely-powdered resin and finely-powdered brick-dust, two spoonfuls each; incorporate the whole well together, and it will hold the metal much faster than plain glue.

To polish brass ornaments inlaid in wood.

If your brass-work be very dull, file it with a small, smooth file; then polish it with a rubber of hat dipped in Tripoli powder mixed with linseed oil, in the same manner as you would polish varnish, until it has the desired effect.

To wash brass figures over with silver.

Take one ounce of aquafortis, and dissolve in it, over a moderate fire, one drachm of good silver, cut small or granulated; this silver being wholly dissolved, take the vessel off the fire, and throw into it as much white tartar as is required to absorb all the liquor. The residue is a paste, with which you may rub over any work made of copper, and which will give it the colour of silver.

To imitate tortoise-shell on copper.

Rub copper laminas over with oil of nuts, then dry them over a slow fire, supported by their extremities upon small iron bars.

PART III.

Dyeing, Staining, Gilding, etc.

OF DYEING AND STAINING WOODS, IVORY, BONE, TORTOISESHELL, MUSICAL INSTRUMENTS, AND ALL OTHER MANUFACTURED ARTICLES; WITH THE PROCESSES OF SILVERING, GILDING, AND BRONZING.

DYEING wood is mostly applied for the purpose of veneers, while staining is more generally had recourse to to give the desired colour to the article after it has been manufactured. In the one case, the colour should penetrate throughout, while in the latter the surface is all that is essential.

In dyeing pear-tree, holly, and beech, take the best black; but for most colours, holly is preferable. It is also best to have your wood as young and as newly cut as possible. After your veneers are cut, they should be allowed to lie in a trough of water for four or five days before you put them into the copper: as the water, acting as a purgative to the wood, brings out abundance of slimy matter, which, if not thus removed, the wood will never be of a good colour. After this purificatory process, they should be dried in the open air for at least twelve hours. They are then ready for the copper. By these simple means, the colour will strike much quicker, and be of a brighter hue. It would also add to the improvement of the colours, if, after your veneers have boiled a few hours, they are taken out, dried in the air, and again immersed in the colouring copper. Always dry veneers in the open air, for fire invariably injures the colours.

Fine black.

Put six pounds of chip logwood into your copper, with as many veneers as it will conveniently hold, without pressing too tight; fill it with water, and let it boil *slowly* for about three hours; then add half a pound of powdered verdigris, half a pound of copperas, and four ounces of bruised nut-galls; fill the copper up with vinegar as the water evaporates; let it boil gently two hours each day till the wood is dyed through.

Another method.

Procure some liquor from a tanner's pit, or make a strong decoction of oak-bark, and to every gallon of the liquor add a quarter of a pound of green copperas, and mix them well together, put the liquor into the copper, and make it quite hot, but not to boil; immerse the veneers in it, and let them remain for an hour; take them out, and expose them to the air till it has penetrated its substance; then add some logwood to the solution, place your veneers again in it, and let it simmer for two or three hours; let the whole cool gradually, dry your veneers in the shade, and they will have acquired a very fine black.

Fine blue.

Into a clean glass bottle put one pound of oil of vitriol, and four ounces of the best indigo pounded in a mortar, (take care to set the bottle in a basin or earthen glazed pan, as it will ferment;) now put your veneers into a copper or stone trough; fill it rather more than one-third with water, and add as much of the vitriol and indigo (stirring it about) as will make a fine blue, which you may know by trying it with a piece of white paper or wood; let the veneers remain till the dye has struck through.

The colour will be much improved, if the solution of indigo in vitriol be kept a few weeks before using it. You will also find the colour strike better, if you boil your veneers in plain water till completely soaked through, and let them remain for a few hours to dry partially, previous to immersing them in the dye.

Another.

Throw pieces of quicklime into soft water; stir it well; when settled, strain or pour off the clear part; then to every gallon add ten or twelve ounces of the best turnsole; put the whole into your copper with your veneers, which should be of white holly, and prepared as usual by boiling in water; let them simmer gently till the colour has sufficiently penetrated, but be careful not to let them boil in it, as it would injure the colour.

A fine yellow.

Reduce four pounds of the root of barberry, by sawing, to dust, which put in a copper or brass trough; add four ounces of turmeric and four gallons of water, then put in as many white holly veneers as the liquor will cover; boil them together for three hours, often turning them; when cool, add two ounces of aquafortis, and the dye will strike through much sooner.

A bright yellow.

To every gallon of water, necessary to cover your veneers, add one pound of French berries; boil the veneers till the colour has penetrated through; add the following liquid to the infusion of the French berries, and let your veneers remain for two or three hours, and the colour will be very bright.

Liquid for brightening and setting colours.

To every pint of strong aquafortis, add one ounce of grain tin, and a piece of sal-ammoniac of the size of a walnut; set it by to dissolve, shake the bottle round with the cork out, from time to time: in the course of two or three days it will be fit for use. This will be found an admirable liquid to add to any colour, as it not only brightens it, but renders it less likely to fade from exposure to the air.

Bright green.

Proceed as in either of the previous receipts to produce a yellow; but instead of adding aquafortis or the brightening liquid, add as much vitriolated indigo (page 59) as will produce the desired colour.

Another green.

Dissolve four ounces of the best verdigris, and sap green and indigo half an ounce each, in three pints of the best vinegar; put in your veneers, and gently boil till the colour has penetrated sufficiently.

The hue of the green may be varied by altering the proportion of the ingredients; and I should advise, unless wanted for a particular purpose, to leave out the sap green, as it is a vegetable colour very apt to change, or turn brown, when exposed to the air.

Bright red.

To two pounds of genuine Brazil dust, add four gallons of water; put in as many veneers as the liquor will cover; boil them for three hours; then add two ounces of alum, and two ounces of aquafortis, and keep it lukewarm until it has struck through.

Another red.

To every pound of logwood chips, add two gallons of water; put in your veneers, and boil as in the last; then add a sufficient quantity of the brightening liquid (page 61) till you see the colour to your mind; keep the whole as warm as you can bear your finger in it, till the colour has sufficiently penetrated.

The logwood chips should be picked from all foreign substances, with which it generally abounds, as bark, dirt, &c.; and it is always best when fresh cut, which may be known by its appearing of a bright red colour; for if stale, it will look brown, and not yield so much colouring matter.

Purple.

To two pounds of chip logwood and half a pound of Brazil dust, add four gallons of water, and after putting in your veneers, boil them for at least three hours; then add six ounces of pearlash and two ounces of alum; let them boil for two or three hours every day, till the colour has struck through.

The Brazil dust only contributes to make the purple of a more red cast; you may, therefore, omit it, if you require a deep blush purple.

Another purple.

Boil two pounds of logwood, either in chips or powder, in four gallons of water, with your veneers, after boiling till the colour is well struck in, add by degrees vitriolated indigo, (see page 59,) till the purple is of the shade required, which may be known by trying it with a piece of paper; let it then boil for one hour, and keep the liquid in a milk-warm state till the colour has penetrated the veneer. This method, when properly managed, will produce a brilliant purple, not so likely to fade as the foregoing.

Orange.

Let the veneers be dyed, by either of the methods given in page 61, of a fine deep yellow, and while they are still wet and saturated with the dye, transfer them to the bright red dye as in page 62, till the colour penetrates equally throughout.

Silver gray.

Expose to the weather in a cast-iron pot of six or eight gallons, old iron nails, hoops, &c., till covered with rust; add one gallon of vinegar, and two of water, boil all well for an hour; have your veneers ready, which must be air-wood, (not too dry,) put them in the copper you use to dye black, and pour the iron liquor over them; add one pound of chip logwood, and two ounces of bruised nut-galls; then boil up another pot of the iron liquor to supply the copper with, keeping the veneers covered, and boiling two hours a day, till of the required colour.

Another gray.

Expose any quantity of old iron, or what is better, the borings of gun-barrels, &c., in any convenient vessel, and from time to time sprinkle them with spirits of salt, (muriatic acid,) diluted in four times its quantity of water, till they are very thickly covered with rust; then to every six pounds add a gallon of water, in which has been dissolved two ounces of salt of tartar; lay your veneers in the copper, and cover them with this liquid: let it boil for two or three hours till well soaked, then to every gallon of liquor add a quarter of a pound of green copperas, and keep the whole at a moderate temperature till the dye has sufficiently penetrated.

STAINING.

Staining wood is altogether a different process from dying it, and requires no preparation before the stain be applied: it is peculiarly useful to bedstead and chair makers. In preparing the stain, but little trouble is required; and, generally speaking, its application differs very little from that of painting. When carefully done, and properly varnished, staining has a very beautiful appearance, and is much less likely to meet with injury than japanning.

Black stain for immediate use.

Boil half a pound of chip logwood in two quarts of water, add one ounce of pearlash, and apply it hot to the work with a brush. Then take half a pound of logwood, boil it as before in two quarts of water, and add half an ounce of verdigris and half an ounce of copperas; strain it off, put in half a pound of rusty steel filings; with this, go over your work a second time.

To stain beech a mahogany colour.

Put two ounces of dragon's blood, broken in pieces, into a quart of rectified spirits of wine; let the bottle stand in a warm place, shake it frequently; when dissolved, it is fit for use.

Another method for a black stain.

Boil one pound of logwood in four quarts of water, add a double handful of walnut-peel or shells; boil it up again, take out the chips, add a pint of the best vinegar, and it will be fit for use; apply it boiling hot.

This will be improved, if, when dry, you apply hot a solution of green copper, as dissolved in water, (an ounce to a quart,) over your first stain.

To imitate rosewood.

Boil half a pound of logwood in three pints of water till it is of a very dark red; add half an ounce of salt of tartar. While boiling hot, stain your wood with two or three coats, taking care that it is nearly dry between each; then, with a stiff flat brush, such as is used by the painters for graining, form streaks with the black stain above-named, which, if carefully executed, will be very nearly the appearance of dark rosewood.

Another method.

Stain with the black stain; and when dry, with a brush as above, dipped in the brightening liquid, (see page 61,) form red veins, in imitation of the grain of rosewood, which will produce a beautiful effect.

A handy brush for the purpose may be made out of a flat brush, such as is used for varnishing; cut the sharp points off, and make the edges irregular, by cutting out a few hairs here and there, and you will have a tool which will accurately imitate the grain.

To imitate king or Botany-bay wood.

Boil half a pound of French berries in two quarts of water, till of a deep yellow, and, while boiling hot, give two or three coats to your work: when nearly dry, form the grain with the black stain, which must also be used hot.

You may, for variety, to heighten the colour, after giving it two or three coats of yellow, give one of strong logwood liquor, and then use the black stain as directed.

Red stain for bedsteads and common chairs.

Archil, as sold at the shops, will produce a very good stain of itself, when used cold; but if, after one or two coats being applied, and suffered to get almost dry, it is brushed over with a hot solution of pearlash in water, it will improve the colour.

To improve the colour of any stain.

Mix in a bottle one ounce of nitric acid, half a tea-spoonful of muriatic acid, a quarter of an ounce of grain tin, and two ounces of rain water. Mix it at least two days before using, and keep your bottle well corked.

To stain horn in imitation of tortoise-shell.

Mix an equal quantity of quicklime and red lead with strong soap lees, lay it on the horn with a small brush, in imitation of the mottle of tortoise-shell; when dry, repeat it two or three times.

To stain ivory or bone red.

Boil shavings of scarlet cloth in water, and add by degrees pearlash till the colour is extracted; a little roach alum, now added, will clear the colour; then strain it through a linen cloth. Steep your ivory or bone in aquafortis (nitrous acid) diluted with twice its quantity of water; then take it out, and put it into your scarlet dye till the colour is to your mind. Be careful not to let your aquafortis be too strong; neither let your ivory remain too long in it. Try it first with a slip of ivory, and if you observe the acid has just caused a trifling roughness on its surface, take it out immediately, and put it into the red liquid, which must be warm, but not too hot. A little practice, with these cautions, will enable you to succeed according to your wishes; cover the places you wish to remain unstained with white wax, and the stain will not penetrate in those places, but leave the ivory of its natural colour.

To stain ivory or bone black.

Add to any quantity of nitrate of silver (lunar caustic) three times its bulk of water, and steep your ivory or bone in it; take it out again in about an hour, and expose it to the sunshine to dry, and it will be a perfect black.

To stain ivory or bone green.

Steep your work in a solution of verdigris and sal-ammoniac in weak aquafortis, in the proportion of two parts of the former to one of the latter, being careful to use the precautions mentioned for staining red, in page 69.

To stain ivory, &c. blue.

Stain your materials green according to the previous process, and then dip them in a strong solution of pearlash and water.

To stain ivory, &c. yellow.

Put your ivory in a strong solution of alum in water, and keep the whole some time nearly boiling; then take them out and immerse them in a hot mixture of turmeric and water, either with or without the addition of French berries; let them simmer for about half an hour, and your ivory will be of a beautiful yellow. Ivory or bone should dry very gradually, or it will split or crack.

TO STAIN MUSICAL INSTRUMENTS.

Fine crimson.

Boil one pound of good Brazil dust in three quarts of water for an hour; strain it, and add half an ounce of cochineal; boil it again gently for half an hour, and it will be fit for use.

If you will have it more of a scarlet tint, boil half an ounce of saffron in a quart of water for an hour, and pass over the work previous to the red stain.

Purple.

To a pound of good chip logwood, put three quarts of water; boil it well for an hour; then add four ounces of pearlash, and two ounces of indigo pounded.

Fine black.

In general, when black is required in musical instruments, it is produced by japanning; the work being well prepared with size and lampblack, apply the black japan, (as sold at the varnish-maker's,) after which, varnish and polish.

But as a black stain is sometimes required for finger-boards, bridges, and flutes, you may then proceed as directed in staining; but the wood ought to be either pear, apple, or boxwood; the latter is preferable; and if it be rubbed over, when dry, with a rag or flannel dipped in hot oil, it will give it a gloss equal to ebony.

Fine blue.

Into a pound of oil of vitriol (sulphuric acid) in a clean glass phial, put four ounces of indigo, and proceed as above directed in dyeing purple.

Fine green.

To three pints of the strongest vinegar, add four ounces of the best verdigris pounded fine, half an ounce of sap green, and half an ounce of indigo.

Distilled vinegar, or verjuice, improves the colour.

Bright yellow.

You need not stain wood yellow, as a small piece of aloes put into the varnish will have all the desired effect.

To stain boxwood brown.

Hold your work to the fire, that it may receive a gentle warmth; then take aquafortis, and with a feather pass over the work till you find a change to a fine brown, (always keeping it near the fire;) you may then oil and polish it.

SILVERING AND GILDING.

The art of silvering, as applied to cabinet-work, is precisely similar to that of gilding; the directions for the one will, therefore, be the instructions for the other, with little other variation than using silver-leaf instead of gold-leaf. Silvering for plate-glass is a trade by itself, and is too troublesome and expensive a process, except where carried on in an extensive way, to be introduced in a work where its place can be occupied with matter more useful to the cabinet-maker.

There are two methods of gilding. That for out-door work, to stand the weather or to wash, is called oil-gilding; this is performed by means of oil or varnish. The other, called burnish-gilding, is the most beautiful, and best adapted for fine work—as frames, articles of furniture, &c., or as applied by the cabinet-maker in the internal decoration of rooms, or the carved work of furniture. Both these methods are so essential to the ingenious workman, that we shall give him every instruction necessary to perform his work in the best manner.

The requisites necessary to be provided with.

First, a sufficient quantity of leaf-gold, which is of two sorts—the deep gold, as it is called, and the pale gold. The former is the best; the latter very useful, and may occasionally be introduced for variety or effect.

Second, a gilder's cushion: an oblong piece of wood, covered with rough calf-skin, stuffed with flannel several times doubled, with a border of parchment, about four inches deep at one end, to prevent the air blowing the leaves about when placed on the cushion.

Thirdly, a gilding-knife, with a straight and very smooth edge, to cut the gold.

Fourthly, several camel-hair pencils in sizes, and tips, made of a few long camel's hairs put between two cards, in the same manner as hairs are put into tin cases for brushes, thus making a flat brush with a very few hairs.

Lastly, a burnisher, which is a crooked piece of agate set in a long wooden handle.

Size for oil gilding.

Grind calcined red-ochre with the best and oldest drying oil, and mix with it a little oil of turpentine when used.

When you intend to gild your work, first give it a coat of parchment-size; then apply the above size where requisite, either in patterns or letters, and let it remain till, by touching it with your fingers, it feels just sticky; then apply your gold-leaf, and dab it on with a piece of cotton; in about an hour wash off the superfluous gold with sponge and water, and, when dry, varnish it with copal varnish.

To make size for preparing frames, &c.

To half a pound of parchment shavings, or cuttings of white leather, add three quarts of water, and boil it in a proper vessel till reduced to nearly half the quantity; then take it off the fire, and strain it through a sieve. Be careful, in the boiling, to keep it well stirred, and do not let it burn.

To prepare frames or wood-work.

First, with the above alone, and boiling-hot, go over your frames in every part; then mix a sufficient quantity of whiting with size, to the consistency of thick cream, with which go over every part of your frame six or seven times, carefully letting each coat dry before you proceed with the next, and you will have a white ground fit for gilding on, nearly or quite the sixteenth of an inch in thickness.

Your size must not be too thick, and, when mixed with the whiting, should not be put on so hot as the first coat is by itself. It will be better to separate the dirty or coarse parts of the whiting by straining it through a sieve. Vauxhall-whiting is the best.

Polishing.

When the prepared frames are quite dry, clean and polish them. To do this, wet a small piece at a time, and, with a smooth, fine piece of cloth, dipped in water, rub the part till all the bumps and inequalities are removed; and for those parts where the fingers will not enter, as the mouldings, &c., wind the wet cloth round a piece of wood, and by this means make the surface all smooth and even alike.

Where there is carved work, &c., it will sometimes be necessary to bring the mouldings to their original sharpness by means of chisels, gouges, &c., as the preparation will be apt to fill up all the finer parts of the work, which must be thus restored. It is sometimes the practice, after polishing, to go over your work once with fine yellow or Roman ochre; but this is rarely necessary.

Gold-size.

Grind fine sal-ammoniac well with a muller and stone; scrape into it a little beef-suet, and grind all well together; after which, mix in with a pallet-knife a small proportion of parchment-size with a double proportion of water.

Another gold-size.

Grind a lump of tobacco-pipe clay into a very stiff paste with thin size; add a small quantity of ruddle and fine black-lead, ground very fine, and temper the whole with a small piece of tallow.

To prepare your frames for gilding.

Take a small cup or pipkin, into which put as much gold-size as you judge sufficient for the work in hand; add parchment-size till it will just flow from the brush; when quite hot, pass over your work with a very soft brush, taking care not to put the first coat too thick; let it dry, and repeat it twice or three times more, and, when quite dry, brush the whole with a stiff brush, to remove any remaining knobs. Your work is now ready for applying the gold.

Your parchment-size should be of such a consistence, when cold, as the common jelly sold in the shops: for if too thick it will be apt to chip, and if too thin it will not have sufficient body.

Laying on the gold.

This is the most difficult part of the operation, and requires some practice; but, with a little caution and attention, it may be easily performed.

Turn your gold out of your book on your cushion, a leaf at a time; then, passing your gilding-knife under it, bring it into a convenient part of your cushion for cutting it into the size of the pieces required; breathe gently on the centre of the leaf, and it will lay flat on your cushion; then cut it to your mind by bringing the knife perpendicularly over it, and sawing it gently till divided.

Place your work before you in a position nearly horizontal, and, with a long-haired camel's-hair pencil, dipped in water, (or with a small quantity of brandy in the water,) go over as much of your work as you intend the piece of gold to cover; then take up your gold from your cushion with your tip; by drawing it over your forehead or cheek, it will damp it sufficiently to adhere to the gold, which must then carefully be transferred to your work, and, gently breathing on it, it will adhere; but take care that the part you apply it to is sufficiently wet; indeed, it must be floating, or you will find the gold apt to crack: proceed in this manner by a little at a time, and do not attempt to cover too much at once, till by experience you are able to handle the gold with freedom. Be careful, in proceeding with your work, if you find any flaws or cracks appear, to take a corresponding piece of gold, and apply it immediately; sometimes, also, you will find it necessary, when your gold does not appear to adhere sufficiently tight, to draw a pencil quite filled with water close to the edge of the gold, that the water may run underneath it, which will answer your expectation.

Burnishing.

When your work is covered with gold, set it by to dry; it will be ready to burnish in about eight or ten hours; but it will depend on the warmth of the room or state of the air, and practice will enable you to judge of the proper time.

When it is ready, those parts which you intend to burnish must be dusted with a soft brush, and, wiping your burnisher with a piece of soft wash-leather, (quite dry,) begin to burnish about an inch or two in length at a time, taking care not to lean too hard, but with a gentle and quick motion apply the tool till you find it equally bright all over.

Matting, or dead gold.

Those parts of your work which look dull from not being burnished, are now to be matted, that is, are to be made to look like dead gold; for if left in its natural state it will have a shining appearance, which must be thus rectified:—

Grind some vermilion, or yellow ochre, very fine, and mix a very small portion either with the parchment-size or with the white of an egg, and with a very soft brush lay it even and smooth on the parts intended to look dull; if well done, it will add greatly to the beauty of the work.

The work must be well cleared of superfluous gold, by means of a soft brush, previous to burnishing or matting.

Finishing.

It is now only necessary to touch the parts in the hollows with a composition made by grinding vermilion, gamboge, and red lead, very fine, with oil of turpentine, and applying it carefully with a small brush in the parts required, and your work is completed.

Sometimes the finishing is done by means of shell-gold, which is the best method; it should be diluted with gum-Arabic, and applied with a small brush.

To make shell-gold.

Take any quantity of leaf-gold, and grind it, with a small portion of honey, to a fine powder; add a little gum-Arabic and sugar-candy, with a little water, and mix it well together; put it in a shell to dry until you want it.

Silver-size.

Take tobacco-pipe clay, grind it fine with a little black lead and Genoa soap, and add parchment-size as directed for the gold-size.

NOTE.—Any soap would most probably answer as well as Genoa soap; but it is here directed, as it has been found to answer very well.

Silvering.

Silvering is at present but little in use, though some old works still look very well, and it might be introduced with advantage to many works; the great fault is that it is apt to tarnish; but may be preserved, with very little diminution to its beauty, by applying a thin coat of the cleanest copal or mastic varnish. The process for silvering is exactly the same as for gilding; but the matting must be done by mixing a small quantity of flake white in a powder, with a little Prussian blue (just sufficient to tinge it) along with plain size or white of egg.

To make liquid foil for silvering glass globes, bent mirrors, &c.

To half an ounce of lead, add half an ounce of fine tin, and melt them together in an iron ladle; when in a state of fusion, add half an ounce of bismuth; skim off the dross, remove the ladle from the fire, and, before it cools, add five ounces of quicksilver, and stir the whole well together, observing not to breathe over it, as the evaporation of the silver is very pernicious.

In mixing, avoid breathing the fumes that are evaporated, as it is a poison of the most deadly nature.

Another method.

To four ounces of quicksilver, put as much tin foil as will become barely fluid when mixed; have your globe clean and warm, and inject the quicksilver by means of a clean earthen pipe at the aperture, turning it about till it is silvered all over; let the remainder run out, and hang it up.

An excellent receipt to burnish gold-size.

One ounce of blacklead, ground very fine, one ounce of deer-suet, one ounce of red chalk, and one pound of pipe-clay, ground with weak parchment-size to a stiff consistency; to be used as directed in the article "Size for oil gilding," page 74.

To gild leather for bordering-doors, folding-screens, &c.

Damp a clear brown sheepskin with a sponge and water, and strain it tight, with tacks, on a board, sufficiently large; when dry, size it with clear double size; then beat the whites of eggs, with a whisk, to a foam, and let them stand to settle; then take books of leaf-silver, a sufficient quantity, and blow out the leaves of silver on a gilder's cushion; pass over the leather carefully with the egg-size, and with a tip-brush lay on the silver, closing any blister with a piece of cotton; when dry, varnish them over with yellow lacker till they are of a fine gold colour. Your skin being thus gilt, you may then cut it into strips as you please, and join with paste to any length.

Perform the foregoing operation in the height of summer, when the air is clear, dry, and warm, that the skin may dry well before you size it, and the size may have the desired effect upon the pores, and no further, and the silver will not tarnish before you lacker it.

To gild the borders of leather tops of library-tables, work-boxes, &c.

The tops of library-tables, &c., are usually covered with Morocco leather, and ornamented with a gilt border, and are usually sent to the bookbinder for that purpose. The method by which they perform it is as follows:—They first go over that part intended to be gilt with a sponge dipped in the glair of eggs, which is the whites beaten up to a froth, and left to settle; and the longer made or older it is so much the better; then, being provided with a brass roller, on the edge of which the pattern is engraved, and fixed as a wheel in a handle, they place it before the fire till heated, so that, by applying a wetted finger, it will just hiss; while it is heating, rub the part with an oiled rag, or clean tallow, where the pattern is intended to be, and lay strips of gold on it, pressing it down with cotton: then with a steady hand run the roller along the edge of the leather, and wipe the superfluous gold off with an oiled rag, and the gold will adhere in those parts where the impression of the roller has been, and the rest will rub off with the oiled rag.

BRONZING.

The art of bronzing is equally useful to the cabinet-maker as the smith—the carved and turned work in furniture being frequently finished in imitation of bronze, and, if well done, has a very elegant effect, and adds much to the beauty of the article. It is by no means a difficult process, but nevertheless requires considerable care and judgment to arrive at perfection.

To bronze figures.

For the ground, after it has been sized and rubbed down in a similar manner as if for gilding, take Prussian blue, verditer, and spruce ochre; grind them separately in water, turpentine, or oil, according to the work; mix them together in such proportions as will produce the colour you desire; then grind Dutch-metal, commonly called bronze, in the same material you grind your colour. laying it on the prominent parts of the figure; and, if done with care, it will produce a grand effect.

There are several different colours of bronze, which are best imitated by the powders sold at almost all colour-shops, called bronze-powders, in dependent of the one here mentioned of Dutch-metal, which it will be best to purchase, as they are made, not without considerable trouble, by dissolving different metals in aquafortis, and precipitating the solutions by means of sal-ammoniac, and washing the precipitate in water, and drying it on blotting-paper. The ingenious artist will suit the colour of the bronze by mixing corresponding colours of paint for a ground.

To bronze on wood.

Having stained those parts intended for bronzing black, by any of those methods shown under the article "Staining," take japanners' gold-size, and mix with a small portion of Roman ochre and Prussian blue; go over the blacked parts lightly; then suffer it to dry till it feels just sticky to the fingers, but not to come off; then, with a hard ball of cotton dipped in any of the bronze powders, rub those places that are prominent, and, if you think proper, give it a thin coat of japanners' gold-size, thinned with spirits of turpentine. Or you may alter the colour of your bronze, by mixing either more or less blue, as also other colours, as verditer green by it.

self; but do not put your colour on thick over the black stain, but rather glaze it on,—for it is not wanted in a body, but should be rather transparent, as it makes it more of a metallic appearance.

To bronze brass figures for ornaments.

After having lackered your brass-work in those parts you wish to look like gold, take for those parts as are intended to appear as bronze any quantity of umber, either burnt or in its natural state, according to the colour you require, and grind it with a small quantity of spirits of wine. Do the same with verditer, and also spruce ochre. Keep these colours separate for use, and, when wanted, take some pale gold-lacker and mix with it a portion of these ingredients till you get the colour required; then apply this mixture in the same manner as directed in lackering brass-work, (page 88.) You may also mix with it any coloured bronze-powder, for the sake of variety. A little experience, and a few experiments with these compositions, will enable the workman to imitate any bronze or colour he pleases.

PART IV.

Lackering, Japanning, Varnishing, &c

OF LACKERING, JAPANNING, VARNISHING, AND POLISHING CABINET AND UPHOLSTERY WORK GENERALLY.

LACKERING.

AMONG the arts that lend their assistance to the cabinet-maker, in the completion of many of his articles of furniture, that of lackering must not be forgotten. To do what the cabinet-maker may require, few directions are necessary, it being a simple and easy process.

To lacker brass-work.

If your work is old, clean it first, according to the directions hereafter given; but if new, it will merely require to be freed from dust, and rubbed with a piece of wash-leather, to make it as bright as possible. Put your work on a hot iron plate (or the hob of your fire-place will be a good substitute) till it is modeately heated, but not too hot, or it will blister your lacker; then, according to the colour you wish, take of the following preparations, and, making it warm, lay hold of your work with a pair of pincers or pliers, and with a soft brush apply the lacker, being careful not to rub it on, but stroke the brush gently one way, and place your work on the hot plate again till the varnish is hard; but do not let it remain too long. Experience will best tell you when it should be removed. Some, indeed, do not place it on the stove or plate a second time. If it should not be quite covered, you may repeat it carefully; and, if pains be taken with your lacker, it will look equal to metal gilt.

To make gold lacker for brass.

Rectified spirits of wine, half a pint; mix half a pound of seed-lac, picked clean, and clear of all pieces (as upon that depends the beauty of the lacker) with the spirits of wine; keep them in a warm place, and shake them repeatedly. When the seed-lac is quite dissolved, it is fit for use.

Another lacker.

Take of the clearest and best seed-lac a quarter of a pound, and of dragon's-blood a quarter of an ounce pound them well together, add a gill and a half of the best spirits of wine, set .t in a warm place to dissolve; strain it, and it is fit for use.

Superior lacker for brass.

Take of seed-lac, three ounces; amber or copal, ground on porphyry, one ounce; dragon's-blood, twenty grains; extract of red sandal-wood, fifteen grains; oriental saffron, eighteen grains; very pure alcohol, twenty ounces. To apply this varnish to ornaments or articles of brass, expose them to a gentle heat, and dip them into the varnish; two or three coatings may be applied in this manner, if necessary. The varnish is durable, and has a beautiful colour. Articles varnished in this manner may be cleansed with water and a bit of dry rag.

Pale gold lacker.

Dissolve, in a quarter of a pint of spirits of wine, as much gamboge as will give it a bright yellow; then add three ounces of seed-lac, finely powdered and sifted; set it in a sand-bath to dissolve. When that is the case, bottle and stop it well till wanted for use.

Lacker with spirits of turpentine.

Take seed-lac two ounces, sandaric or mastic

two ounces, dragon's-blood a quarter of an ounce, gum gutte twenty grains, clear turpentine one ounce, and the best spirits of turpentine sixteen ounces.

This lacker, though certainly not equal to those made with spirits of wine, is, from its cheapness, often very useful for the more common purposes. It does not dry so quick, nor is it so durable; but for such purposes as lackering silvered leather, &c., it answers very well. We may here remark that we may vary the colour of our lackers by using more or less, or altering the proportion of the colouring material; and at the same time notice that all the colouring substances that are of a resinous quality, or that will give out their colouring matter when infused in spirits, are proper to be used in the composition of lacker. We may therefore make lackers of almost any colour, by selecting different colouring materials, and mixing them with the other compositions used as the basis of all lackers, such as seed-lac, shell-lac, &c.

To clean old brass-work for lackering.

Make a strong ley of wood-ashes, which may be strengthened by soap-lees; put in your brass-work, and the lacker will soon come off; then have ready a mixture of aquafortis and water, sufficiently strong to take off the dirt; wash it afterwards in clean water, and lacker it with such of the above compositions as may be most suitable to your work.

JAPANNING.

JAPANNING is generally performed by persons brought up to the practice of the art exclusively; but, as it frequently happens that japanned work receives damage when it is very inconvenient (either for distance or other circumstances) to send for a japanner to repair it, it may not be improper to lay down the most simple methods used in that branch.

Take care to provide yourself with a small muller and stone, to grind any colour you may require; and observe that all your wood-work must be prepared with size, and some coarse material mixed with it, to fill up and harden the grain of the wood, (such as may best suit the colour intended to be laid on,) which must be rubbed smooth with glass paper when dry; but in cases of accident, it is seldom necessary to re-size the damaged places, unless they are considerable.

Always grind your colours smooth in spirits of

turpentine; then add a small quantity of turpentine and spirit-varnish; lay it carefully on with a camel's-hair brush, and varnish it with brown or white spirit-varnish, according to the colour.

You will also find a box, filled with currier's shavings, useful for cleaning your stones and pallet with, for they should never be laid by dirty, as the beauty of the work depends a great deal on keeping all your colours separated: therefore, before you grind another colour, the first should be well wiped off your stone.

For a black japan.

Mix a little gold-size and lampblack: it will bear a good gloss without varnishing over.

To imitate black rosewood.

The work must be grounded black, after which well grind some red lead, mixed up as before directed, which lay on with a flat stiff brush, in imitation of the streaks in the wood: after which, take a small quantity of lake, ground fine, and mix it with brown spirit-varnish, carefully observing not to have more colour in it than will just tinge the varnish: but, should it, on trial, be still too red, assist it with a little umber ground very fine, with which pass over the whole of the work intended to imitate black rosewood, and it will have the desired effect.

If well done, when it is varnished and polished it will scarcely be known from rosewood.

Instead of the umber in the above, you may use a small quantity of Vandyke brown; it is much more transparent than the umber.

INDIA JAPANNING.

The great peculiarity in the Indian method is the embossing, or raising the figures, &c., above the surface or ground, and the metallic or bronze-like hue of the several designs; the grotesque appearance of the several ornaments, whether figures, landscapes, or whatever other designs they are embellished with, being so totally different from every principle of perspective, and so opposite to every idea we have of correct drawing. Nothing but the study of Chinese models themselves will enable the workmen to imitate, with any degree of precision, their several characteristics. We can, therefore, only give such directions for preparing the ground, embossing the designs, and producing the peculiar effect of Chinese japan, as will enable the ingenious mechanic to execute any work of the kind with truth and accuracy, according to any copy given, while it must remain with him to use taste and judgment in effecting a likeness which will characterize this peculiar manufacture.

Ground for Chinese japan.

Mix any quantity of the finest whiting to the consistency of paint with isinglass size; lay on your wood two or three coats, observing to put it on evenly and smoothly, and not too thick; let it dry; then rub it gently with a soft rag and water till the surface is quite level and polished; if you add a small portion of honey to the mixture, it will render it less liable to crack or peel off. If your ground is to be black, which is the most usual one, give it a coat or two of the black japan mentioned in the common method of japanning, and it is prepared for your figures, &c.

Another ground.

Mix fine plaster of Paris with size not too thick and apply it quickly, for it soon gets hard. Two coats, in most instances, will be sufficient. After it is quite dry, polish it with fine glass paper, and rub it with a wet soft cloth; then give it two or three coats of drying linseed oil, or as much as it will soak up. When dry, it is ready for japanning.

To make black japan.

Grind ivory or lampblack very fine with turpentine, add a little lac varnish or copal varnish, and temper it to a proper consistency with varnish for laying on your ground. Give your work two or three coats at least, using a gentle heat, as directed in varnishing.

To trace your designs on the ground.

Having drawn the figures on a piece of white paper either with ink or pencil, rub the back of it with fine chalk or whiting, and shake all the loose powder off: lay it on your ground, and trace or go over every part of your outline with the end of a blunt bodkin, or other similar instrument; you will then have a sketch in faint outline on your ground. You may then proceed to put in your figures, &c., with any colour you wish, or bronze them.

To raise figures on your work.

Prepare a mixture of whiting and size, (some prefer the whites of eggs,) of a consistency to flow freely from your pencil, the hairs of which must be rather long. Begin with a figure, or other part —but do not do too much at a time—and trace the outline correctly, with a free hand; then take a piece of stick pointed at the end, dip it into your composition, and fill up the inside of your outline. Continue to put more of the mixture on till it is raised sufficiently above the surface. Let it get quite dry, and then polish it with a small camel's-hair pencil and clean water, so as to make it perfectly smooth and level. Care must be taken in this process, that your composition is not too thin, or it will spread beyond the bounds of your outline,—but just so thick as to drop from the stick. Some mix with the whiting a portion of flake-white, or dry white-lead. This is an improvement, and for very particular work should be adopted.

BRONZES PECULIARLY ADAPTED FOR INDIA JAPANNING AND SIMILAR PURPOSES.

Gold.

PUT any quantity of gold-leaf into a stone mortar, together with a small portion of honey and a little water; grind them well together, till the gold seems dispersed throughout the whole paste; add by degrees more water till it is quite thin, keeping it continually stirred; let it settle, and pour the water off, as near as you can, without wasting your gold; repeat the washing till you see the gold in the form of a fine powder at the bottom. Then pour the water clean off, and turn the gold out on a piece of blotting-paper; keep it from the dust, and, when all the moisture is evaporated, put it into a bottle for use.

This is a very expensive bronze, and used only for those works which are very particular. But a very good substitute may be had by treating Dutch-metal in the same manner; but be sure to keep this close-stopped, or it is very apt to tarnish.

Copper.

Put some very fine filings of copper into an iron mortar, and beat them the same as that of the gold-leaf or Dutch-metal; instead of using honey, you may pound it dry with a portion of sal-ammoniac, and then wash it as above; keep this also from the air. Brass filings may be treated in the same manner.

Silver

May be made with silver-leaf, treated in the same manner as directed for gold. This must also be kept well stopped in a bottle, and wrapped in paper, as it is as apt to change as the Dutch-metal.

Tin.

Melt grain-tin in a ladle over the fire; when in a fluid state, add, by degrees, quicksilver, and stir it well. It will be transformed into a grayish powder, which, for the sake of variety, you may use with others, either alone or mixed.

By mixing these different bronzes together, you may produce a great variety, that will add much to the beauty of your work; and we may here remark, that there is a variety of colours in gold-leaf, all of which will produce a differently coloured powder.

In the city, a variety of coloured bronzes can be procured at the colour shops, at less expense than we can make them: but not so in the country. We have, therefore, here set down those that are most generally useful.

Method of applying the bronze.

Go over the part you intend to bronze with gold-size or varnish; when it is sufficiently dry—that is, when it does not adhere to the finger, but feels clammy— dip a piece of cotton, rolled into a hard ball, in your bronze-powder, and dab it on the place to be bronzed.

To japan work-boxes, &c.

There is a very pretty method of ornamenting boxes, cabinets, &c., so that the figures appear of the colour of the wood, and the ground black; this, by many, is produced by first tracing out the pattern, and then pricking-in those parts which shall appear as the ground, either black or any colour at fancy. This is a very tedious process, and even when finished with the greatest care, will not appear regular or well defined in the pattern. The following method will be found very expeditious, and at the same time very correct; it is but little known, and, as such, will to the practical japanner be the more acceptable. It may also be applied to many other purposes than here alluded to. The following preparation is necessary, and may be termed *the stopping out mixture;* it is made by dissolving the best white beeswax in spirits of turpentine till it is of the consistency of varnish. Keep this mixture in a bottle, and, when wanted for use, mix sufficient for your present purpose with white lead in powder, or flake-white, to give it a body—but not too thick, only so that it will flow freely from your pencil. Having traced your design, go over those parts which you wish to remain of the colour of your wood, and let it dry; then mix ivory-black, in very fine powder, with parchment or isinglass-size, and go evenly and smoothly over every part of your work. It will now appear wholly black, or of whatever colour you have mixed with your size. Let the whole get thoroughly dry; then, with a stiff brush dipped in plain spirits of turpentine, rub the whole of the work well, and those parts that have been gone over with the stopping-out mixture, will come off, leaving your black or other colour perfect. It will then appear as if you had pricked-in your work, but much more sharp, and will, if carefully done, have a beautiful effect. You have now nothing more to do than varnish your work, as in general, and polish it as directed under the article Polishing, page 113.

In finishing your work in the manner of Indian japan, you must not be sparing of your varnish, but give it eight or ten coats, so that it will bear polishing.

Sealing-wax varnish.

For fancy work, this has of late years been much used, and, if well applied and your wax good, will be a very good imitation of India japan. The method of making the varnish or japan is very easy, being simply reducing the wax to a coarse powder, and pouring the best spirits of wine on it in a bottle, and letting it gradually dissolve without heat, shaking the bottle occasionally till it is all dissolved. A two-ounce stick of the best wax will be enough for a quarter of a pint of spirits.

Recollect that much depends on the goodness of the sealing-wax, and that you may vary the colour of the varnish by using differently coloured wax. As this varnish dries very quickly, it should not be made until it is wanted for use.

VARNISHING.

Of late years, varnishing has arrived at a state of perfection which enables the workman of the present day to finish his work in a style far superior to any thing previously known. By the help of this useful auxiliary, he can heighten the beauty of fine wood, and give additional lustre to furniture. The simplicity of the process requires but little to be said on the subject; but we shall endeavour, as clearly as possible, to lay down some rules and cautions necessary to be observed, both in the making and method of using varnish, that the work may appear as beautiful as possible.

In the city, it is hardly worth while to make varnish, unless in large quantities, as there are several shops where it may be had very good, and at a fair price; but in the country, where the carriage is an object, and you cannot depend upon the genuineness of the article, it is necessary to be known by the practical mechanic; yet, where it can be purchased, we should recommend it to be had. The varnish generally sold for varnishing furniture is white hard varnish.

Cautions respecting the making of varnish.

As heat in many cases is necessary to dissolve the gums used in making varnish, the best way, when practicable, is to use what the chemists call a sand-bath, which is simply placing the vessel in which the varnish is in another filled with sand and placed on the fire. This will generally be sufficient to prevent the spirits catching fire; but to avoid such an accident, (which not unfrequently happens,) it will be best to take a vessel sufficiently large that there shall be little danger of spilling its contents; indeed, the vessel should never be more than two-thirds filled. However, a piece of board sufficiently large to cover the top of the vessel should always be at hand in case the spirits should take fire; as also a wet wrapper, in case it should be spilt, as water itself thrown on would only increase the mischief. The person who attends the varnish-pot should have his hands covered with gloves, and, if they are made of leather and rather damp, it will effectually prevent injury. These cautions should be well observed, or shocking personal injury may result from their neglect.

General directions in choosing gums and spirits.

In purchasing gum, examine it, and see that it consists for the most part of clear, transparent lumps, without a mixture of dirt. Select the clearest and lightest pieces for the most particular kinds of varnish, reserving the others, when separated from extraneous matter, for the coarser varnishes. In choosing spirits of wine, the most simple test is by immersing the finger in it; if it burns quickly out, without burning the finger, it is good; but if, on the contrary, it is long in burning, and leaves any dampness remaining on the finger, it is mixed with inferior spirit. It may be also compared with other spirit, by comparing the weight of equal quantities; the lightest is the best. The goodness of spirits of turpentine may be likewise ascertained in the same manner by weighing it, and by noticing the degree of inflammability it possesses. The most inflammable is the best; and a person much in the habit of using it will tell by the smell its good or bad qualities; for good turpentine has a pungent smell, and the bad a very disagreeable one, and not so powerful.

To varnish a piece of furniture.

First make the work quite clean; then fill up all knots or blemishes with cement of the same colour. See that your brush is clean, and free from loose hairs; then dip it in the varnish, stroke it along the wire raised across the top of your varnish-pot, and give the work a thin and regular coat; soon after that, another, and another, always taking care not to pass the brush twice in the same place. Let it stand to dry in a moderately warm place, that the varnish may not chill.

When you have given your work about six or seven coats, let it get quite hard, (which you will prove by pressing your knuckles on it; if it leave a mark, it is not hard enough;) then, with the first three fingers of your hand, rub the varnish till it chafes, and proceed over that part of the work you mean to polish, in order to take out all the streaks or partial lumps made by the brush; then give it another coat, and let it stand a day or two to harden.

The best vessel for holding varnish is sold at colour-shops, called a varnish-pan. It is constructed of tin, with a false bottom; the interval between the two bottoms is filled with sand, which, being heated over the fire, keeps the varnish fluid, and it flows more readily from the brush. There is a tin handle to it, and the false bottom comes sloping from one end to the other, which causes the varnish to run to one end. It has also a wire fixed across the top, to wipe the brush against.

To make the best white hard varnish.

Rectified spirits of wine, one quart; gum sandarac, ten ounces; gum mastic, two ounces; gum anime, half an ounce; dissolve these in a clean can, or bottle, in a warm place, frequently shaking it. When the gum is dissolved, strain it through a lawn sieve, and it is fit for use.

To keep brushes in order.

The brushes used for varnishing are either flat in tin, or round, tied firm to the handle, and made either of camel's-hair or very fine bristles. It is necessary to be very careful in cleaning them after being used; for, if laid by with the varnish in them, they are soon spoiled. Therefore, after using, wash them well in spirits of wine or turpentine, according to the nature of your varnish; after which, you may wash them out with hot water and soap, when they will be as good as new, and last a great while with care. The spirits that are used for cleaning may be used to mix with varnish for the more common purposes, or the brushes may be cleaned merely with boiling water and strong yellow soap.

Mastic varnish for pictures or drawings.

To one pint of spirits of turpentine put ten ounces of the clearest gum mastic; set the mixture in a sand-bath till it is all dissolved; then strain it through a fine sieve, and it is ready for use. If too thick, thin it with spirits of turpentine.

Turpentine varnish.

To one pint of spirits of turpentine add ten ounces of clear resin, pounded; put the mixture in a tin can, on a stove, and let it boil for half an hour. When the resin is all dissolved, let it cool, and it is fit for use.

Varnishes for violins, &c.

To one pint of rectified spirits of wine put one ounce and a half of gum mastic, and one-third of a gill of turpentine varnish; keep the mixture in a very warm place, in a tin can, frequently shaking it until dissolved; then strain it, and keep it for use. If it is harder than you wish, add a **little** more turpentine varnish.

To varnish drawings, or any kind of paper or card work.

Boil clear parchment-cuttings in water, in a clean glazed pipkin, till they produce a very clear size; strain the mixture, and keep it for use.

Give any work two coats of the above size, passing quickly over it, so as not to disturb the colours; proceed as before directed (page 105) with your varnish.

A still better method.

Dissolve one ounce of the best isinglass in about a pint of water, by simmering it over the fire: strain it through fine muslin, and keep it for use.

Try the size on a piece of paper moderately warm. If it glistens, it is too thick; add more water. If it soaks into the paper, it is too thin; add or diminish the isinglass till it merely dulls the surface. Then give your drawing two or three coats, letting it dry between each, being careful (particularly in the first coat) to bear very lightly on the brush, (which should be a flat tin camel's-hair,) from which the size should flow freely; otherwise, you may damage the drawing.

Then take the best mastic varnish, and with it give at least three coats, and the effect will answer your most sanguine wishes.

This is the method used by many eminent artists, and is found superior to any that has been tried.

Amber varnish.

To eight ounces of amber, in powder, add two of gum-lac; melt the amber, in a glazed pipkin, with half a pint of the best spirits of turpentine; and, when melted, add the gum-lac. Place it again on the fire, and keep stirring it with a piece of wood till all is dissolved; then add one ounce of the clearest cold-drawn linseed-oil; stir it well together, and strain it for use.

Oil varnish.

Boil one pint of the best linseed-oil an hour; then add a quarter of a pound of the clearest resin in powder; stir it well till dissolved; add one ounce of spirits of turpentine; strain it, and bottle for use.

This is a cheap and good varnish for sash frames, or any work where economy is required. It has besides, the property of bearing hot water without being damaged, and is not subject to scratch,

Copal varnish.

Take spirits of wine one pint, gum-copal half an ounce, and shell-lac one-fourth of an ounce: reduce the gums to powder; put the spirits in a jar or bottle; add the gums. Place the whole in a warm place, with the cork lightly in the bottle; shake it occasionally, and, when the gums are quite dissolved, strain, and bottle for use.

To make a colourless copal varnish.

As all copal is not fit for this purpose, to ascertain such pieces as are good, each must be taken separately, and a single drop of pure essential oil of rosemary, not altered by keeping, must be let fall on it. Those pieces that soften at the part that imbibes the oil are good. Reduce them to powder, which sift through a very fine hair sieve, and put into a glass, on the bottom of which it must not lie more than a finger's-breadth thick; pour upon it essence of rosemary to a similar height; stir the whole for a few minutes, when the copal will dissolve into a viscous fluid. Let it stand for two hours, and then pour gently on it two or three drops of very pure alcohol, (spirits of wine,) which distribute over the oily mass by inclining the bottle in different directions with a very gentle motion. Repeat this operation by little and little till the incorporation is effected, and the varnish reduced to a proper degree of fluidity. It must then be left to stand a few days, and, when clear, may be decanted off for use.

This varnish, thus made without heat, may be applied with equal success to pasteboard, wood, and metals, and takes a better polish than any other. It may be used on paintings, the beauty of which it greatly heightens.

Turpentine copal varnish.

To one ounce and a half of gum-copal add eight ounces of the very best oil of turpentine; put the turpentine into a vessel, in a sand-bath, when it is very hot: but be cautious not to let it boil. Then gradually add the gum-copal, stirring it with a wooden spatula, adding fresh gum as the other dissolves. When all is thoroughly incorporated, take the vessel off the bath, and put it to cool; let it remain covered over for a few days to settle, and decant it clear off.

In making this varnish, it frequently happens that the gum will not melt so readily as it ought, which, in general, is owing to the turpentine not being sufficiently rectified; but, when that is good, it will always succeed. It is best also to let your turpentine be exposed for some time in the sun, in a corked bottle, that the watery particles may be gradually dissipated. The bottle should not be stopped quite tight.

A varnish which suits all sorts of prints and pictures, stands water, and makes the work appear as shining as glass.

Dilute one quarter of a pound of Venice turpentine with a gill, or thereabouts, of spirits of wine. If too thick, a little more of the latter: if not enough, a little more of the former; so that you bring it to the consistence of milk. Lay one coat of this on the right side of the print, and, when dry, it will shine like glass. If it be not to your liking, you may lay on another coat.

To make appear in gold the figures of a print.

After having laid on both sides of the print one coat of the above-described varnish, in order to make it transparent, let it dry a little while; then, before it is quite so, lay some gold in leaves on the wrong side of the print, pressing it gently on with the cotton you hold in your hand. By these means, all parts whereon you shall lay these leaves will appear like true massive gold on the right side.

When this is all thoroughly dry, lay on the right side of it one coat of the varnish described above and it will then be as good as any crown glass. You may also put a pasteboard behind the print, to support it better in its frame.

Method of preparing the composition used for coloured drawings and prints, so as to make them resemble paintings in oil.

Take of Canada balsam one ounce, spirit of turpentine two ounces; mix them together. Before this composition is applied, the drawing or print should be sized with a solution of isinglass in water, and, when dry, the varnish should be applied with a camel's-hair brush.

POLISHING.

The beauty of cabinet-work depends upon the care with which it is finished. Some clean off with scraping and rubbing with glass-paper. This should be done in all cases; but it is not enough, particularly where the grain is anyways soft. A good glass-paper also is essential, (directions for making which will be found in our miscellaneous receipts.) A polish should then be added. But, unless the varnish for cabinet-work be very clear and bright, it will give a dingy shade to all light-coloured woods. This should, therefore, be a previous care.

Again, some workmen polish with rotten stone, others with putty-powder, and others with common whiting and water; but Tripoli will be found to answer the best.

To polish varnish

Is certainly a tedious process, and considered by many as a matter of difficulty.

Put two ounces of powdered Tripoli into an earthen pot or basin, with water sufficient to cover it; then with a piece of fine flannel four times doubled, laid over a piece of cork rubber, proceed to polish your varnish, always wetting it well with the Tripoli and water. You will know when the process is complete by wiping a part of the work with a sponge, and observing whether there is a fair and even gloss. Clean off with a bit of mutton-suet and fine flour.

CAUTION.—Be careful not to rub the work too hard, or longer than is necessary to make the face perfectly smooth and even.

The French method of polishing.

With a piece of fine pumice-stone, and water,

pass regularly over the work with the grain until the rising of the grain is down; then, with powdered Tripoli and boiled linseed oil, polish the work to a bright face. This will be a very superior polish, but it requires considerable time.

To polish brass ornaments inlaid in wood.

The brass-work must first be filed very even with a smooth file; then, having mixed some Tripoli powdered very fine, with linseed oil, with a rubber made from a piece of old hat or felt, polish the work as you would polish varnish, until the desired effect is produced.

If the work be ebony, or black rosewood, take some elder-coal, powdered very fine, and apply it dry after you have done with the Tripoli. It will increase the beauty of the polish.

To polish ivory.

If ivory be polished with putty-powder and water. by means of a rubber made of hat, it will in a short time produce a fine gloss.

To polish any work of pearl.

Go over it with pumice-stone, finely powdered, (first washed to separate the impurities and dirt,) with which you may polish it very smooth; then apply putty-powder as directed for ivory, and it will produce a fine gloss and a good colour.

To polish marble.

It sometimes happens that the cabinet-maker has a table-top of marble to remount, which is scratched, and requires re-polishing. The following is the process used by the mason, and will, therefore, be acceptable in a work like the present. With a piece of sandstone with a very fine grit, rub your slab backward and forward, using very fine sand and water, till the marble appears equally rough, and not in scratches; next use a finer stone and finer sand, till its surface appears equally gone over; then, with fine emery-powder and a piece of felt or old hat wrapped round a weight, rub it till all the marks left by the former process are worked out, and it appears with a comparative gloss on its surface. Afterward, finish the polish with putty-powder and fine, clean rags. As soon as the face appears of a good gloss, do not put any more powder on your rags, but rub it well, and in a short time it will appear as when fresh out of the mason's hands.

To polish tortoise-shell or horn.

Having scraped your work perfectly smooth and

level, rub it with very fine sand-paper or Dutch rushes; repeat the rubbing with a bit of felt dipped in a very finely powdered charcoal with water, and, lastly, with rotten-stone or putty-powder; and finish with a piece of soft wash-leather, damped with a little sweet oil.

FRICTION VARNISHING, OR FRENCH POLISHING.

The method of varnishing furniture, by means of rubbing it on the surface of the wood, is of comparatively modern date. To put on a hard face, which shall not be so liable to scratch as varnish, and yet appear equally fine, the French polish was introduced; and it would be unpardonable in a work like this to omit a full direction of the process, and also the various preparations of the different compositions necessary.

All the polishes are used much in the same way. A general description will therefore be a sufficient guide for the workman. If your work be porous, or the grain coarse, it will be necessary to give it a coat of clear-size previous to your commencing with the polish; and, when dry, gently go over it with very fine glass-paper. The size will fill up the pores, and prevent the waste of the polish, by being absorbed into the wood, and be also a saving of considerable time in the operation.

Make a wad with a piece of coarse flannel or drugget, by rolling it round and round, over which, on the side meant to polish with, put a very fine linen rag several times doubled, to be as soft as possible; put the wad or cushion to the mouth of the bottle containing the preparation, (or polish,) and shake it, which will damp the rag sufficiently; then proceed to rub your work in a circular direction, observing not to do more than about a square foot at a time; rub it lightly till the whole surface is covered; repeat this three or four times, according to the texture of the wood. Each coat is to be rubbed until the rag appears dry; and be careful not to put too much on the rag at a time, and you will have a very beautiful and lasting polish. Be also very particular in letting your rags be very clean and soft, as the polish depends, in a great measure, on the care you take in keeping it clean and free from dust during the operation.

The true French polish.

To one pint of spirits of wine add a quarter of an ounce of gum-copal, a quarter of an ounce of gum-Arabic, and one ounce of shell-lac.

Let your gums be well bruised, and sifted through

a piece of muslin. Put the spirits and the gums together in a vessel that can be closely corked, place them near a warm stove, and frequently shake them. In two or three days they will be dissolved. Strain the mixture through a piece of muslin, and keep it tight corked for use.

Another French polish.

Take one ounce each of mastic, sandaric, seed-lac, shell-lac, gum-lac, and gum-Arabic; reduce them to powder, and add a quarter of an ounce of virgin-wax; put the whole into a bottle, with one quart of rectified spirits of wine; let it stand twelve hours, and it will be fit for use.

To apply it, make a ball of cloth and put on it occasionally a little of the polish; then wrap the ball in a piece of calico, which slightly touch with linseed oil. Rub the furniture hard with a circular motion, until a gloss is produced; finish in the same manner, but, instead of all polish, use one-third polish to two-thirds spirits of wine.

Or, put into a glass bottle one ounce of gum-lac, two drachms of mastic in drops, four drachms of sandaric, three ounces of shell-lac, and half an ounce of gum-dragon; reduce the whole to powder; add to it a piece of camphor the size of a nut, and pour on it eight ounces of rectified spirits of wine. Stop the bottle close, but take care, when the gums are dissolving, that it is not more than half full. It may be placed near a gentle fire, or on a German stove; but a bath of hot sand is preferable, as avoiding all danger, the compound being so very apt to catch fire. Apply it as before directed.

An improved polish.

To a pint of spirits of wine add, in fine powder, one ounce of seed-lac, two drachms of gum-guaiacum, two drachms of dragon's-blood, and two drachms of gum-mastic; expose them, in a vessel stopped close, to a moderate heat for three hours, until you find the gums dissolved; strain the whole into a bottle for use, with a quarter of a gill of the best linseed oil, to be shaken up well with it.

This polish is more particularly intended for dark-coloured woods—for it is apt to give a tinge to light ones, as satin-wood, or air-wood, &c.—owing to the admixture of the dragon's-blood, which gives it a red appearance.

Water-proof polish.

Take a pint of spirits of wine, two ounces of gum-benzoin, a quarter of an ounce of gum-sandaric, and a quarter of an ounce of gum-anime;

these must be put into a stopped bottle, and placed either in a sand-bath or in hot water till dissolved; then strain the mixture, and, after adding about a quarter of a gill of the best clear poppy oil, shake it well up, and put it by for use.

Bright polish.

A pint of spirits of wine to two ounces of gum-benzoin and half an ounce of gum-sandarac, put in a glass bottle corked, and placed in a sand-bath or hot water until you find all the gum dissolved, will make a beautiful clear polish for Tunbridge-ware goods, tea-caddies, &c. It must be shaken from time to time, and, when all dissolved, strained through a fine muslin sieve, and bottled for use.

Prepared spirits.

This preparation is useful for finishing after any of the foregoing receipts, as it adds to the lustre and durability, as well as removes every defect, of the other polishes; and it gives the surface a most brilliant appearance.

Half a pint of the very best rectified spirits of wine, two drachms of shell-lac, and two drachms of gum-benzoin. Put these ingredients in a bottle, and keep it in a warm place till the gum is all dissolved, shaking it frequently; when cold, add two tea-spoonfuls of the best clear white poppy oil, shake them well together, and it is fit for use.

This preparation is used in the same manner as the foregoing polishes; but, in order to remove all dull places, you may increase the pressure in rubbing.

Strong polish.

To be used in the carved parts of cabinet-work with a brush, as in standards, pillars, claws, &c.

Dissolve two ounces of seed-lac and two ounces of white resin in one pint of spirits of wine.

This varnish or polish must be laid on warm, and, if the work can be warmed also, it will be so much the better; at any rate, moisture and dampness must be avoided.

Directions for cleaning and polishing old furniture.

Take a quart of stale beer or vinegar, put a handful of common salt and a table-spoonful of spirits of salt into it, and boil it for a quarter of an hour; you may keep it in a bottle, and warm it when wanted for use. Having previously washed your furniture with soft hot water, to get the dirt off, wash it carefully with the above mixture; then polish, according to the directions, with any of the foregoing polishes.

PART V.
Glues, Cements, &c.

OF GLUES, CEMENTS, WAXES, AND COMPOSITIONS FOR FILLING UP AND ORNAMENTING CABINET AND UPHOLSTERY WORK; AND MISCELLANEOUS RECEIPTS.

CEMENTS.

To make mahogany-coloured cement.

MELT two ounces of beeswax and half an ounce of resin together; then add half an ounce of Indian red, and a small quantity of yellow ochre, to bring the cement to the desired colour; keep it in a pipkin for use.

Portable glue, or bank-note cement.

Boil one pound of the best glue, strain it very clear; boil also four ounces of isinglass; put it into a double glue-pot, with half a pound of fine brown sugar, and boil it pretty thick; then pour it into plates or moulds. When cold, you may cut and dry them for the pocket.

This glue is very useful to draughtsmen, architects, &c., as it immediately dilutes in warm water, and fastens the paper without the process of damping: or, it may be used by softening it in the mouth, and applying it to the paper.

Cement for turners.

Melt together beeswax one ounce, resin half an ounce, and pitch half an ounce; stir in the mixture some very fine brickdust to give it a body. If too soft, add more resin; if too hard, more wax. When nearly cold, make it up into cakes or rolls, which keep for use.

This will be found very useful for fastening any piece of wood on your chuck, which is done by applying your roller of cement to the chuck, and it will adhere with sufficient force.

A cement for broken glass.

Steep one ounce of isinglass in half a pint of spirits of wine for twenty-four hours; then let it dissolve over a slow fire, (always keeping it covered, or the spirit will evaporate;) now well bruise six cloves of garlic in a mortar, put them in a linen cloth, and squeeze the juice into the isinglass; mix all well together, and keep it for use. It is excellent to join glass ornaments, &c.

A cement to stop flaws or cracks in wood of any colour.

Put any quantity of fine sawdust of the same wood your work is made with into an earthen-pan, and pour boiling water on it, stir it well, and let it remain for a week or ten days, occasionally stirring it; then boil it for some time, and it will be of the consistence of pulp or paste; put it into a coarse cloth, and squeeze all the moisture from it. Keep for use, and, when wanted, mix a sufficient quantity of thin glue to make it into a paste; rub it well into the cracks, or fill up the holes in your work with it. When quite hard and dry, clean your work off, and, if carefully done, you will scarcely discern the imperfection.

A cement for joining China, &c.

Beat the whites of eggs well to a froth, let them settle, add soft grated or sliced cheese and quick-lime; beat them well together, and apply a little to the broken edges. This cement will endure both the fire and water.

Another cement.

Pound half an ounce of resin and four ounces of gum-mastic; put them into a pipkin on the fire to melt; stir them well. To this add about half an ounce of finely-powdered glass, and half an ounce of quicklime; stir the whole well together. When nearly cold, form it into sticks, on a stone, in the same manner as sticks of sealing-wax are formed When you want to cement any article, heat the broken edges sufficiently to melt your cement, which rub thinly on both edges; bring them accurately together; press them close, and let them cool. If this be carefully done, your work will sooner break in any other part than where the cement has been applied.

A strong glue that will resist moisture.

Dissolve gum-sandarac and mastic, of each a quarter of an ounce, in a quarter of a pint of spirits of wine, to which add a quarter of an ounce of clear turpentine: now take strong glue, or that in which isinglass has been dissolved; then, putting the gums into a double glue-pot, add by degrees the glue, constantly stirring it over the fire till the whole is well incorporated: strain it through a cloth, and it is ready for use. You may now return it into the glue-pot, and add half an ounce of very finely-powdered glass; use it quite hot. If you join two pieces of wood together with it, you may, when perfectly hard and dry, immerse it in water; and the joint will not separate.

Another glue for the same purpose.

To two quarts of skimmed milk add half a pound of the best glue; melt them together, taking care they do not boil over, and you will have a very strong glue, which will resist damp or moisture.

To make paste for laying cloth or leather on tabletops.

To a pint of the best wheaten flour add resin, very finely powdered, about two large spoonfuls; of alum, one spoonful, in powder; mix them all well together, put them into a pan, and add by degrees soft or rain water, carefully stirring it till it is of the consistence of thinnish cream; put it into a saucepan over a clear fire, keeping it constantly stirred, that it may not get lumpy. When it is of a stiff consistence, so that the spoon will stand upright in it, it is done enough. Be careful to stir it well from the bottom, for it will burn if not well attended to. Empty it out into a pan and cover it over till cold, to prevent a skin forming on the top, which would make it lumpy.

This paste is very superior for the purpose, and adhesive. To use it for cloth or baize, spread the paste evenly and smoothly on the top of the table, and lay your cloth on it, pressing and smoothing it with a flat piece of wood; let it remain till dry; then trim the edges close to the cross-banding. If you cut it close at first, it will, in drying, shrink and look bad where it meets the banding all round. If used for leather, the leather must be first previously damped, and then the paste spread over it; then lay it on the table, and rub it smooth and level with a linen cloth, and cut the edges close to the banding with a short knife. Some lay their table-cover with glue instead of paste, and for cloth perhaps it is the best method; but for leather it is not proper, as glue is apt to run through. In using it for cloth, great care must be taken that your glue is not too thin, and that you rub the cloth well down with a thick piece of wood made hot at the fire, for the glue soon chills. You may, by this method, cut off the edges close to the border at once.

MISCELLANEOUS RECEIPTS.

Glass paper.

TAKE any quantity of broken window-glass, (that which has rather a green appearance on the edge is best;) pound it in an iron mortar; then have two or three sieves, of different degrees of fineness, ready for use when wanted. Take any good, tough paper, (fine cartridge is the best,) level the knobs and bumps on both sides with pumice-stone, tack it at each corner on a board, and, with good, clear glue, diluted with about one-third more water than is used generally for wood-work, go quickly over the paper, taking care to spread it even with your brush; then, having your sieve ready, sift the pounded glass over it lightly, yet so as to cover it in every part; let it remain till the glue is set; take it from the board, shake off the superfluous glass into the sieve, and hang it in the shade to dry In two or three days it will be fit for use.

This paper will be much better than any you can buy, sand being frequently mixed with the glass, and coloured, to deceive the purchaser.

To clean the face of soft mahogany or other porous wood.

After scraping and sand-papering in the usual manner, take a sponge and well wet the surface, to raise the grain; then, with a piece of fine pumice-stone, free from stony particles and cut the way of the fibres, rub the wood in the direction of the grain, keeping it moist with water. Let the work dry; then, if you wet it again, you will find the grain much smoother, and it will not raise so much. Repeat the process, and you will find the surface perfectly smooth, and the texture of the wood much hardened. By this means, common soft Honduras mahogany will have a face equal to fine Hispaniola.

If this does not succeed to your satisfaction, you may improve the surface by using the pumice-stone with cold-drawn linseed oil, in the same manner as you proceeded with water. This will be found to give a most beautiful as well as a durable face to your work, which may then be polished or varnished.

Another way to clean and finish mahogany work.

Scrape and sand-paper your work as smooth as possible; go over every part with a brush dipped in furniture-oil, and let it remain all night; have ready the powder of the finest red brick, which tie up in a cotton stocking, and sift equally over the work the next morning, and, with a leaden or iron weight in a piece of carpet, rub your work well the way of the grain, backward and forward, till it has a good gloss. If not sufficient, or if the grain appears any way rough, repeat the process. Be careful not to put too much of the brick-dust, as it should not be rubbed dry, but rather as a paste upon the cloth. When the surface is perfectly smooth, clean your work off with a rubber of carpet and fine mahogany sawdust. This process will give a good gloss and face to your work, and make a surface that will improve by wear. Indeed, by this process, soft Honduras mahogany will have the appearance of Spanish.

To darken light mahogany.

In repairing old furniture, it frequently happens that we cannot match the old wood. Therefore, after the repairs are completed, to prevent the pieces introduced looking like patches, wash them with soap-lees, or dissolve quicklime in water, and use in the same manner; but be careful not to let either be too strong, or it will make the wood too dark, it is best, therefore, to use it rather weak at first, and, if not dark enough, repeat the process till the wood is sufficiently darkened.

To cut good steel scrapers.

Part of the blade of a broken saw makes the best scrapers; but, as it is hard, it is very difficult to cut it into the required form. The best and most expeditious way is to mark it out to the size wanted, and then to place the blade or steel plate in a vice whose chaps shut very close, placing the mark even with the face of the vice, and the part to be cut to waste above the vice. Then with a cold-chisel, or a common steel-firmer that has its basil broken off, holding it close to the vice and rather inclined upwards, begin at one end of the steel plate, and with a sharp blow of the hammer it will cut it. Keep going on by degrees, and you will with ease cut it to the shape required; then grind the edges of your scraper level, and finish by rubbing it on your Turkey-stone.

To sharpen and set a saw.

First, run a file along the edge of the teeth till you see them range in a direct line; then lay the blade on a smooth piece of lead, or on the end of your trying-plane, and with a square steel punch give a gentle tap on it with a hammer; after placing it on one of the teeth, do the same with every alternate tooth. Reverse the saw and punch the teeth on the other side, and look down your saw that the teeth are all equally set. Then begin with your file at that part of your saw nearest the handle. To sharpen or file the teeth to a good point, hold your file so that it makes an angle with the saw-blade of about thirty degrees, or two-thirds that of a mitre angle, observing to shift the file for every alternate tooth in an opposite inclination, bringing each tooth to a very sharp point, and keeping the upper edge of your file very nearly horizontal. Every tooth will then represent a sharp chisel, and cut as it goes without tearing.

To take bruises out of furniture.

Wet the part with warm water; double a piece of brown paper five or six times, soak it, and lay it on the place; apply on that a hot flat-iron till the moisture is evaporated. If the bruise be not gone, repeat the process. After two or three applications, the dent or bruise will be raised level with the surface. If the bruise be small, merely soak it with warm water, and apply a red-hot poker very near the surface; keep it continually wet, and in a few minutes the bruise will disappear.

To make anti-attrition.

According to the specification of the patent, this mixture is made of one part of plumbago or blacklead ground very fine, and four parts of hog's lard or grease, mixed well together. It prevents the effects of friction much better than oil or other grease, and is very useful to the turner, and will be found to make the lathe work much easier, as well as to be a great saving in oil, which with constant use grows stiff, and sensibly impedes the motion; while this preparation, once applied, will last a long time without requiring renewal.

Polish for turners' work.

Dissolve sandarac in spirits of wine in the proportion of one ounce of sandarac to half a pint of spirits; next shave beeswax one ounce, and dissolve it in a sufficient quantity of spirits of turpentine to make it into a paste; add the former mixture by degrees to it; then with a woollen cloth apply it to the work while it is in motion in the lathe, and with a soft linen rag polish it. It will appear as if highly varnished.

To clean and restore the elasticity of cane chair bottoms, couches, &c.

Turn up the chair bottom, and with hot water and a sponge wash the cane-work, so that it may be thoroughly soaked. Should it be dirty, use a little soap. Let it dry in the air, and it will be as tight and firm as when new, provided the cane be not broken.

To clean silver furniture.

Lay the furniture, piece by piece, upon a charcoal fire, and, when they are just red, take them off and boil them in tartar and water, and your silver will have the same beauty as when first made.

To clean marble, sienna, jasper, porphyry, or scagliola.

Mix the strongest soap-lees with quicklime, to the consistency of milk; let it lay on the stone, &c., for twenty-four hours; then clean it off, and wash with soap and water, and it will appear as new.

This may be improved by rubbing or polishing it afterward with fine putty-powder and olive oil.

To take ink-spots out of mahogany.

Apply spirits of salts with a rag until the spots disappear, and immediately afterward wash with clear water.

Another method.

To half a pint of soft water put an ounce of oxalic acid and half an ounce of butter of antimony; shake it well, and when dissolved it will be very useful in extracting stains from mahogany, as well as ink, if not of too long standing.

To make furniture paste.

Scrape two ounces of beeswax into a pot or basin; then add as much spirits of turpentine as will moisten it through. At the same time, powder an eighth part of an ounce of resin, and add to it, when dissolved to the consistence of paste, as much Indian red as will bring it to a deep mahogany colour. Stir it up, and it will be fit for use.

Another method.

Scrape two ounces of beeswax as before; then to half a pint of spirits of turpentine, in a clean glazed pipkin, add half an ounce of alkanet-root; cover it close, and put it over a slow fire, attending it carefully, that it may not boil or catch fire.

When you perceive the colour to be drawn from the root, by the liquid being of a deep red, add as much of it to the wax as will moisten it through; at the same time, add the eighth part of an ounce of powdered resin; cover it close, and let it stand six hours, and it will be fit for use.

To make furniture oil.

Put linseed-oil into a glazed pipkin, with as much alkanet-root as it will cover; let it boil gently till it becomes of a strong red colour; let it cool, and it will be fit for use.

Another method.

Boil together cold-drawn linseed oil, and as much alkanet-root as it will cover, and to every pint of oil add one ounce of the best rose pink. When all the colour is extracted, strain it off, and to every pint add half a gill of spirits of turpentine. This will be a very superior composition for soft and light mahogany.

Black wax

Is made of one ounce of beeswax to half an ounce of Burgundy pitch; melt them together, and add one ounce and a half of ivory-black, ground very fine, and dried.

Green wax.

Melt one ounce of beeswax, and add half an ounce of verditer; let the pipkin be large enough, as the wax will immediately boil up. Stir it well, and add the eighth part of an ounce of resin, when it will be sufficiently hard and fit for use.

To take out spots of oil or grease from cloth.

Drop on the spot some oil of tartar, or salt of wormwood, which has been left in a damp place till it turns into a fluid; then immediately wash the place with lukewarm soft water, and then with cold water, and the spot will disappear.

This will be found very useful, as it frequently happens that the cloth of the card tables, and the inside flaps of secretaries, are spotted and greasy. By proceeding as above, every spot of grease will be completely taken out.

To make parchment transparent.

Soak a thin skin of parchment in a strong ley of wood ashes, often wringing it out till you find it becomes transparent; then strain it on a frame, and let dry.

This will be much improved if, after it is dry, you give it a coat, on both sides, of clear mastic varnish, diluted with spirits of turpentine.

To take out wax spots from cloth or silk.

Put on each spot a piece of soft soap, and place it in the sun, or gently warm it before the fire; let it remain for some time; then wash off with soft water, and the spot will have disappeared.

Another method.

Drop spirits of turpentine or spirits of wine on the spot; then with a sponge rub it gently; repeat it till the spot disappears.

To soften ivory.

Slice a quarter of a pound of mandrake, and put it into half a pint of the best vinegar, into which put your ivory; let the whole stand in a warm place for forty-eight hours, when you will be able to bend the ivory to your mind.

To bleach ivory.

Take a double handful of lime, and slake it by sprinkling it with water; then add three pints of water, and stir the whole together; let it settle ten minutes, and pour the water into a pan for your purpose. Then take your ivory, and steep it in the lime-water for twenty-four hours, after which boil it in a strong alum water one hour, and dry it in the air.

To solder or weld tortoise-shell or horn.

Provide yourself with a pair of pincers or tongs, so constructed that you can reach four inches beyond the rivet; then have your tortoise-shell filed clean to a lap-joint, carefully observing that there is no grease about it; wet the joint with water, apply the pincers hot, following them with water, and you will find the shell to be joined as if it were one piece.

To clean carpets or tapestry.

Your carpet being first well beaten and freed from dust, tack it down to the floor; then mix half a pint of bullock's-gall with two gallons of soft water; scrub it well with soap and the gall-mixture; let it remain till quite dry, and it will be perfectly cleansed, and look like new, as the colours will be restored to their original brightness. The brush you use must not be too hard, but rather long in the hair, or you will rub up the nap and damage the article.

To make composition ornaments for picture-frames or other purposes.

Mix as much whiting as you think will be required for present use with thinnish glue, to the consistence of putty; and, having a mould ready, rub it well all over with sweet oil, and press your composition in it; take it out, and you will have a good impression, which you may set by to dry; or, if wanted, you may, before it gets hard, apply it to your work with thick glue, and bend it into the form required.

If you have not a mould at hand, you may make one of the composition, from any leaf or pattern you may wish to copy, and, letting it get hard, use it as a mould, first oiling it well.

You will find this composition of great use for copying any pattern from good moulds.

To clean pictures.

Having taken the picture out of the frame, take a clean towel, and, making it quite wet, lay it on the face of your picture, sprinkling it from time to time with clean, soft water; let it remain wet for two or three days; take the cloth off, and renew it with a fresh one. After wiping your picture with a clean wet sponge, repeat the process till you find all the dirt soaked out of your picture; then wash it with a soft sponge, and let it get quite dry; rub it with some clear nut or linseed oil, and it will look as well as when freshly done.

Another method.

Put into two quarts of strong ley a quarter of a pound of Genoa soap, rasped very fine, with a pint of spirits of wine; let them simmer on the fire for half an hour, then strain them through a cloth. Apply the preparation with a brush to the picture, wipe it off with a sponge, and apply it a second time, which will remove all dirt. Then, with a little nut-oil warmed, rub the picture, and let it dry. This will make it look as bright as when it came out of the artist's hand.

To silver clock-faces, the scales of barometers, &c.

Take half an ounce of old silver-lace, and an ounce of the best nitric acid; put them in an earthen pot, and place them over a gentle fire till all is dissolved, which will happen in about five minutes; then take the mixture off, and mix it in a pint of clear water, after which pour it into another vessel and free it from sediment; then add a spoonful of common salt, and the silver will be precipitated in the form of a white powder or curd; pour off the acid, and mix the curd with two ounces of salt of tartar, half an ounce of whiting, and a large spoonful of salt; mix it up together, and it is ready for use.

In order to apply the above composition, clean your brass or copper plate with some rotten-stone and a piece of old hat; rub it with salt and water with your hand; then take a little of the composition on your finger and rub it over your plate, and it will firmly adhere, and completely silver it; wash it well with water; when dry, rub it with a clean rag, and varnish it.

This silver is not durable, but may be improved by heating the article and repeating the operation till the covering seems thick enough, or by varnishing it in the following manner:—

Varnish for clock-faces, &c.

Take of spirits of wine one pint; divide it into three parts; mix one part with half an ounce of gum-mastic, in a bottle by itself; one part of spirits, and half an ounce of sandarac in another bottle; and one part of spirits, and half an ounce of the whitest part of gum-benjamin; mix, and temper to your mind: if too thin, some mastic; if too soft, some sandarac or benjamin. When you use it, warm the silvered plate before the fire, and, with a flat camel's-hair pencil, stroke it over till no white streaks appear, and this will preserve the silvering for many years.

Crystallized tin.

Take the best sheet-tin, and the most thickly covered with the metal you can get; clean it well with whiting and water, till the face is well polished; warm it, or lay it on a hot plate, and with a sponge or brush wet it well with strong spirits of salts You will soon see it shoot into beautiful patterns. As soon as this happens, plunge it into cold spring-water. You may then varnish it with any colour you please, or leave it in its natural state, and varnish with clear varnish.

This has of late been much introduced into furniture, and, when well executed, has a beautiful appearance. You may use it as a veneer in the manner of buhl-work, having first given the side you intend to be glued to your work a good coat of paint.

To render plaster figures very durable.

Set a figure in a warm place to get thoroughly dry; then have a vessel large enough to contain it, which so fill that, when the plaster figure is placed in it, it will be quite covered with the best and clearest linseed oil, just warm; let it remain in the vessel for twelve or fourteen hours; then take it out, let it drain, and set it in a place away from dust; and when the oil is quite dry, the ornament, or whatever is thus prepared, will look like wax, and will bear washing without injury.

To make transparent or tracing-paper.

Dissolve a piece of white beeswax, about the size of a walnut, in half a pint of spirits of turpentine; then, having procured some very fine white, woven tissue-paper, lay it on a clean board, and, with a soft brush dipped in this liquid, go over one side, and then turn it over, and apply it to the other; hang it up in a place free from dust, to dry. It will be ready for use in a few days. Some add a small quantity of resin, or use resin instead of wax.

This will be found very useful to the workmen for copying any ornaments or figures, as, by merely laying it on the work, you can trace every line with a pencil, and, if you please, copy it correctly on paper, at your leisure. Or, if it is a pattern for buhl-work, you may paste your tracing-paper on the work you wish to cut, and follow your pattern, as directed under the article Buhl-work. It will be also found very handy for copying sketches or drawings.

To gild metal, by dissolving gold in aqua-regia.

Dissolve gold in aqua-regia, and into the solution dip linen rags; take them out and dry them gently; then burn them to tinder. After you have well polished your work with this, take a cork, and, dipping it into common salt and water, and afterwards into the tinder, rub your work well, and its surface will be gilt.

Aqua-regia is compounded of two parts of nitric acid (aquafortis) and one part of muriatic acid, (spirits of salt,) mixed together.

To silver ivory.

Pound a small piece of nitrate of silver (lunar caustic) in a mortar, add soft water to it, and mix them well together; keep the mixture in a phial for use. When you wish to silver any ivory article, immerse it in this solution, and let it remain till it turns of a deep yellow; then place it in clear water, and expose it to the rays of the sun. Or, if you wish to depicture a figure or cipher on your ivory, dip a camel's-hair pencil in the solution, and draw the subject on the ivory. After it has turned a deep yellow, wash it well with water, and place it in the sunshine, occasionally wetting it with pure water.

In a short time it will turn of a black colour, which, if well rubbed, will change to a brilliant silver.

To clean mirrors, looking-glasses, &c.

Take a soft sponge, wash it well in clean water, and squeeze it as dry as possible; dip it into some spirits of wine, and rub over the glass; then have some powder-blue tied up in a rag, dust it over your glass, and rub it lightly and quickly with a soft cloth; afterward finish with a silk handkerchief.

To clean ormolu ornaments.

When the expense of regilding these ornaments is an object, the following method will, in a great measure, restore them to their original beauty; but, if very much worn, the only way is to take off what remains of the original gilding, and clean them well by immersing them in aqua-regia, or a mixture of muriatic acid and aquafortis, and repeating the original process, which is similar to that of gilding buttons. However, if not in a very bad state, let your ornaments lay some little time in a weak mixture of aquafortis, and then wash them directly in water; lay them on your hot plate, and, when sufficiently heated, apply very pale gold-lacker, and they will look very well, as what remains of the original gilding will not be injured by the aquafortis, though the other parts, as well as the gold, will be perfectly cleansed from every dirt or tarnish.

A green paint for garden-stands, Venetian blinds, trellises, &c.

Take mineral green, and white-lead ground in turpentine; mix up the quantity you wish with a small quantity of turpentine-varnish. This serves for the first coat. For the second, put as much varnish in your mixture as will produce a good gloss. If you desire a brighter green, add a small quantity of Prussian blue, which will much improve the beauty of the colour.

To preserve wood against injury from fire.

Put into a pot an equal quantity of finely pulverized iron-filings, brickdust, and ashes; pour over them glue-water or size; set the whole near the fire, and, when warm, stir them well together. With this liquid wash over all the wood-work which may be in danger, and on its getting dry give it a second coat, when it will be proof against damage by fire.

To remove stains in tables.

Wash the surface with stale beer or vinegar: the stains will then be removed by rubbing them with a rag dipped in spirits of salts. To re-polish, proceed as you would do with new work.

If the work be not stained, wash the surface with clean spirits of turpentine, and re-polish it with furniture-oil.

Hints in melting and using glue.

The hotter the glue, the more force it will exert in keeping the two parts glued together; therefore, in all large and long joints, the glue should be applied immediately after boiling. Glue loses much of its strength by frequent re-melting; that glue, therefore, which is newly made, is much preferable to that which has been re-boiled.

To renew a polished surface.

When furniture has been finished with wax composition, the polish may be renewed by repeating the original process of the wax composition with a small quantity carefully rubbed off.

To clean off the surface of solid work.

First, smooth it with a finely-set smoothing-plane,

and reduce the ridges by a scraper; then rub the surface with glass-paper, finishing it with the finest kind. If the wood be of an open grain, you must, in addition to the above, wet the surface uniformly with a wet sponge, and, when it is dry, rub it a second time with glass-paper, till sufficiently smooth.

Or, while the surface is wet, rub it with pumice-stone in the direction of the fibres; when it becomes dry, wet it again, and the grain will be raised in a less degree than by the first wetting. The rubbing being again repeated, the surface will be found to be still more compact, and susceptible of a much finer polish.

To clean lackered work in brass furniture.

If the stain or blemish be not too deeply seated, washing it with a soft linen or muslin rag wetted with warm water, will remove it. If this does not succeed, you have no resource but to re-lacker.

To cast ornaments or moulding to resemble wood.

Make a very clear cement of five parts of Flanders glue and one part of isinglass, by dissolving the two kinds separately in a large quantity of water; then, after having separated those parts which could not be dissolved, by straining them through fine linen, mix them together. The glue thus prepared must be so heated that the finger can barely endure the temperature; a little water is thus evaporated, and the glue acquires more consistence. Mix raspings of wood or sawdust, passed through a fine sieve, with the glue, forming it into a paste. Having rubbed the plaster or sulphur mould with linseed or nut-oil, as in plaster casts, put in the paste, and press the parts by hand, so that no vacuity may remain; and, in order that the whole may acquire a perfect form, cover it with an oiled board, and place a weight on it. When the cast is dry, remove the rough parts; if any inequalities remain, they are to be smoothed. The ornament thus prepared may be fixed with glue to the article intended.

Cement stopping.

Mix equal quantities of sawdust, of the same wood required to be stopped, and clear glue; and with this stop up the holes or defects of the wood. Where the surface is to be japanned or painted, whiting may be used instead of sawdust. Be sure to let the stopping dry before you attempt to finish the surface.

To clean a veneered surface.

Having scraped away the glue, tooth the surface in an oblique direction to the fibres, and, in proportion as the surface requires regularity, set the plane finer. The final part of the operation of planing is accomplished by a fine tooth plane. Remove all the marks of the tooth plane by a scraper, and finish the surface with glass-paper, or with pumice-stone and glass-paper. Veneers, being of a closer texture than solid wood generally, do not require so much labour as open-grained solid wood.

Grease or dirt in French polish

May be readily removed by rubbing it quickly over with a little spirit of turpentine; which, if carefully done, will not soften the varnish.

Directions in the choice of tools.

With respect to choosing the tools used in the cabinet trade, the most necessary are planes, saws, and chisels. We will consider them first with respect to the wood of which they are manufactured; and secondly the steel which forms their cutting edges. Beech is, in general, and should be always used for the stocks, handles, &c., as it is of a tough texture, and not so liable to split or warp as other woods. There are two kinds of beech, usually known by the names of black and red beech, and the white beech. The former is by far the best in every respect, and may be always known by its colour and texture, which are darker and harder. The white is more apt to warp, and soon wears with use; it should therefore always be rejected as improper. If you examine a piece of beech endwise, you will perceive the grain runs in streaks, which among workmen is called the *beat* of the wood; in all planes, this grain or beat, which is the hard fibrous particle of the wood, runs in a direction perpendicular to the face of the plane, which in that case appears full of little hard specks; whereas, if the beat runs parallel to the face, it will appear in irregular streaks, which situation of the grain should always be avoided, as the face will be apt to wear uneven, and more subject to warp and twist. In saw-handles, and stocks for bits, the beat should run in the same direction as the saw-blade, or in the same direction as the stock, when laid on its side. In moulding-planes, it is very frequently the case that pieces of boxwood are let into that part of the face that forms the quirk of the mouldings; but this, when possible, should never be done, as the two woods are very different, and the different temperature of the atmosphere will cause a difference in the contraction, and consequently the plane will be liable to cast. If it is at any time necessary, introduce a small piece just at the mouth of the plane, firmly dovetailed in, which will not be so apt to derange the accuracy of the plane.

The temper of saws, chisels, and other edged tools.

The quality of the steel should be uniform throughout; indeed, it is always better to have them tempered rather too hard than soft, for use will reduce the temper. If at any time it is necessary to perform the operation yourself, the best method is to melt a sufficient quantity of lead to immerse the cutting part of the tool in. Having previously brightened its surface, plunge it into the melted lead for a few minutes, till it gets sufficiently hot to melt a candle, with which rub its surface; then plunge it in again, and keep it there till the steel assumes a straw colour; but be careful not to let it turn blue. When that is the case, take it out, rub it again with the tallow, and let it cool. If it should be too soft, wipe the grease off, and repeat the process without the tallow; and, when it is sufficiently hot, plunge it into cold spring-water, or water and vinegar mixed. By a proper attention to these directions, and a little practice, every workman will have it in his power to give a proper temper to the tools he may use. If a saw is too hard, it may be tempered by the same means; but as it would be not only expensive, but, in many cases, impossible to do it at home, a plumber's shop is mostly at hand, where you may repeat the process when they are melting a pot of lead. But here observe that the temper necessary is different to other cutting tools: you must wait till the steel just begins to turn blue, which is a temper that will give it more elasticity, and, at the same time, sufficient hardness.

APPENDIX

WOOD STAINING.

The art of "grounding" and "engraving," *i. e.*, imparting various ground shades and fibril figures to wooden surfaces, is both chemical and mechanical.

Staining was formerly subdivided into four parts, namely, "washing," "matching," "imitating," and painting;" but modern stainers have recently added a fifth part, which they term "improving"

WASHING

Consists in coating common white deal or fir with a dilute aqueous solution of clear glue, suitably tinted with a proper combination of two or more of the cheap coloring materials.

For a mahogany color: one part red lead or Venitian red, with two parts yellow lead, chrome, or ochre.

For the antique hues of old wainscot oak: equal parts of burnt umber and brown ochre.

For the shades of rosewood: Venetian red, tinted with lampblack.

For ebony: ivory black.

For the tones of light yellowish woods: whiting or white lead, tinted with orange chrome.

For walnut: burnt umber, modified with yellow ochre.

Wash-color should always be applied in a warm state, by means of a flannel; and the colored wood ought to be evenly wiped dry with shavings or rags

MATCHING

Is the rendering of different pieces of wood, in an article of furniture, of a uniform color, so that they may represent the appearance of one entire piece. To perform a task of this kind successfully, I sometimes treat the various portions in the following manner: I first bleach the darkest parts, by carefully coating them with a strong solution of oxalic acid in hot water, to which are added a few drops of spirit of nitre. When the blanched parts become dry, I coat them two or three times with white polish, by means of a camel-hair pencil. This process, however, does not always prove satisfactory, so I frequently lay on a delicate coat of white stain, and another of white varnish; I then give the intermediate dark parts a coat of common varnish, and proceed to oil all the untouched white portions; next, to compare the whole, and when the white pieces happen to be much lighter than the dark ones, I immediately render them of the exact hue, by coating them with a darkening stain.

The "darkeners" in general use are logwood, lime, brown soft soap, dyed oil, aquafortis, sulphate of iron, nitrate of silver with exposure to the sun's rays, carbonate of soda, bichromate of potash, and many more preparations of an acidulous or alkaline nature. Of these "darkeners" the two last mentioned are the most preferable; and here are the best modes of preparing and using either of them: Procure an ounce of one of these alkalies; powder and dissolve it in two gills of boiling water; next, get three bottles, label them 1, 2, 3, or, *weak, medium, strong;* put one-half of the solution into No. 3, and half a gill into No. 2, and the same into No. 1; then pour an additional gill of clean water into No. 2, and two gills of the same into No. 1. By dissolving both alkalies separately, in the manner described, you will have six liquids, capable of staining nearly all kinds of wood of a complete variety of brown and dark tints.

The solutions of carbonate are generally used for dark materials, like rosewood: and those of the bichromate are applicable to all the intermediate and white woods, such as mahogany, oak, beech, etc.

Here is the safest mode of using these alkaline fluids: Pour a sufficient quantity into a teacup or saucer, into which dip a sponge or a flannel, saturate it thoroughly, then rub evenly over the wood, and terminate by instantly drying off the stained surface with a handful of rags or other soft waste, remembering all the while that, to ensure success, you must follow out this manipulation with the greatest carefulness and the utmost dispatch.

When the dark and light portions are neither very black nor very white, I commonly varnish the former, and allow the latter *to stand in oil* for a time ; by this last means I easily match the different portions of my work, without having recourse to either blanching or staining.

IMPROVING.

An aqueous decoction of barberry root, or an alcoholic solution of gamboge or turmeric, will, when judiciously applied, impart a pleasing yellow hue Oily decoctions of alkanet root, and alcoholic solutions of dragon's blood, yield rich mild reds. Rectified naphtha, that has been dyed with camwood dust, serves for another reddening tincture. Lightest hardwood, such as birch, is frequently improved in color by being sponged with oil, slightly tinted with rose madder, or Venitian red. When these tinctures are used in moderation, they invariably improve the appearance of the grain, and brighten the general tone of ground, so peculiar to many kinds of wood; but few men of any taste whatever will admire a deep red dye upon fine wood.

A solution of asphaltum, in spirit of turpentine, makes a good brown stain for coarse oaken work, which is only intended to be varnished with boiled oil. When discolored ebony has been sponged once or twice with a strong decoction of gall-nuts, to which a quantity of steel dust has been added, its natural blackness becomes more intense The naturally pale ground and obscure grain of Honduras mahogany is often well brought out by its being coated first with spirits of hartshorn, and then with red oil. Grayish maple may be whitened by the process already described in matching. Half a gallon of water, in which half a pound of oak bark and the same quantity of walnut shells or peels have been thoroughly boiled, makes an excellent improver of inferior rosewood; it is also far before any other of its kind for bringing out to perfection the veiny figures and ground shades of walnut. Raw oil, mixed with a little spirit of turpentine, is universally allowed to be the most efficacious improver of the greater number of materials. Beautiful artificial graining may be imparted to various specimens of timber, by means of a camel-hair pencil, with raw oil alone; that is, certain portions may be coated two or three times very tastefully, so as to resemble the rich varying veins which constitute the fibril figures; while the common plain parts, which constitute the ground shades, may only be once coated with the oil very much diluted with spirit of turpentine.

PAINTING

Is rarely employed with satisfaction; but it frequently happens that the polisher makes slight omissions in coloring and staining, which he does not readily perceive until the varnishing or polishing is nearly finished, and in such cases he must either use paint or do his work over again. A box containing the following colours will therefore prove of great atility: Drop black, raw and burnt umber, Vandyke brown, French Naples yellow, cadmium yellow, madder carmine, flake white, and light red. These pigments should be finely pounded, and, when required, they are to be consistently mixed with thin "slake." The objections to painting are that it obscures the natural beauty of the wood, and when, by the effects of time, the properly-stained portions become of a very dark colour, the painted parts invariably retain their artificial hues. Instead of covering the imperfect parts, by an immoderate use of pigments, I often tinge them with dyed polishes and varnishes; and these preparations can be stained black, with logwood, gall-nuts, and copperas; red, with alkanet roots, or camwood dust; yellow, with turmeric, or gamboge; and brown, with carbonate of soda, and a very small quantity of dragon's blood

IMITATIONS.

When curly-veined birch and beech have been regularly brushed with aquafortis, and dried at the fire, they both look remarkably like mahogany. A decoction of logwood and fustic, when put on in a tepid state, produces a similar effect.

The common French mode of effecting an exact representation of the color of mahogany is as follows: First, the white timber is brushed with a dilute solution of nitrous acid; secondly, it is coated once or twice with finishing spirit, in which a quantity of carbonate of soda and dragon's blood have been dissolved (the proper proportions to one gill of spirit being three-fourths of an ounce of the soda and a quarter of an ounce of the blood); the wood is afterwards finished with varnish or polish of a reddish-brown tint. In producing this shade of color, London artisans frequently use a rich brownish-red kind of chalk, the color of which is similar to that of fine Hispaniola mahogany. It is commonly applied in the form of a dry powder by means of a brush, and then well rubbed with another brush or coarse flannel.

Ingenious stainers can make American ash resemble oak wainscot, both in vein and shade, so correctly, as to baffle the most experienced connoisseurs in distinguishing the genuine from the spurious. Some make a commencement by sketching out, upon certain parts of the ashen exterior, the requisite white veins, by means of a camel-hair pencil, with white stain; that done, they coat the veins with thin varnish, and then darken the general ground, dealing carefully throughout the entire process with the veined portions. Others stain and embody, *i. e.*, French polish the ash with the ordinary preparation, after which they pursue an operative course termed "champing;" that is, scratching fancifully, so as to form the veins, upon different parts of the coated surface, before it gets time to harden, with a saturated rag. The former process is, however, the more suitable of the two.

The best mode of producing a representation of oak wainscot upon white materials like beech and fir, consists as follows: A coat of Stephens' satinwood stain is regularly laid on, then a soft graining comb is gently drawn along the stained space, and when the streaks are all correctly produced, the veins are formed with white stain This last coloring stuff is made by digesting three-quarters of an ounce of pearl white (subnitrate of bismuth), and an ounce of isinglass, both of which are sold by the druggist, in two gills of boiling water. The tone of this stain may be modified by being diluted with water, or tinted with other stains.

Showy elmwood, after being delicately darkened, passes in appearance for Italian walnut.

A single coat of No. 3 chromate of potash solution, as previously mentioned, will cause highly-colored and wildly-figured mahogany to resemble rich rosewood so exactly that the best judges may be deceived by it.

To imitate the lively contour and rich ground of rosewood upon inferior white wood, you must produce the ground shade by sponging with a decoction of Braziletto, or Brazil-wood, and the fibril veins by brushing partially and judiciously with black liquor, which is prepared by boiling logwood chips, sulphate of iron, and steel filings, in equally proportioned quantities of vinegar and water. Sometimes a graining comb is passed over the ground shade longitudinally, and with a slight vibratory motion, so as to effect natural-looking streaks, previous to the pencilling or veing.

The appearance of ebony may be given to any species of wood, by the application of three distinct coats of black liquor; and after being smoothed, the counterfeit ebony may be embodied with white polish; this greatly helps to preserve the transparent density of the dyed material.

Of the several compositions and imitative preparations that are sold ready-made, the oak, mahogany, satinwood, rosewood, and ebony powders, sold by Mr. Henry Stephens, 18 St. Martin's le-Grand, London, are unquestionably the most superior. They are all soluble in boiling water, and are much employed for various kinds of joinery, as they form good substitutes for expensive oil paints. Notwithstanding their superiority, the virtues of these dye stuffs may be very much enhanced by the addition of a mordant that is capable of modifying and fastening the tints and shades which they impart. I have successfully employed the following mordants: Spirits of nitre for the satinwood stain; a powerful solution of oxalic acid for the oak; dilute nitrous acid for the mahogany, and No. 3 carbonate solution for the rosewood stains.

Equal proportions of Stephens' oak stain, and No. 2 bichromate solution, constitute a perfect dye stuff, which, when skillfully applied, causes lively-figured beech, birch, or fir, to bear a striking resemblance to dark walnut. By the substitution of aquafortis for the potash, white timber may be converted into counterfeit walnut also, or a mixture composed of similar parts of the acid and alkali, without the oak stain, will answer the same purpose much better, especially if it is to be applied upon American fir.

DIRECTIONS FOR STAINING.

There is no fixed principle upon which certain peculiar tints or shades can be produced, owing, in a great degree, to the natural qualities of wood being so very numerous and variable. The stainer is therefore merely recommended to adhere as much as he possibly can to the following rules : In preparing any of the tinctures already named, it is of some importance to powder or mash all the dry stuffs, previous to dissolving or macerating them, and to purify all the liquids, by filtration, before use. Their coloring powers, which mainly depend on very accurate combinations of the requisite ingredients, should always be carefully tested before a free use be made of them, and the absorbent properties of the materials intended to be stained should be tested.

It will be better for experienced hands to coat two or three times with a weak stain, than only once with a very strong one, as, by the adoption of the first mode, a particular tint may be gradually effected, whereas, by pursuing the latter course, an irremediable discoloration may perhaps prove the consequence.

Coarse pieces of carving, spongy end, and cross-grained woods, should be previously prepared for the reception of stain ; this is best done by putting on a thin layer of varnish, letting it dry, and then glass-papering it completely off again. Fine work merely requires to be oiled and slightly rubbed with the finest glass-paper. Thus prepared, the woody fibre is enabled to take on the stain more regularly, and to retain a high degree of smoothness.

When stain is put on with a flat hog-hair tool, it is improved by a skillful but moderate application of a badger-hair softener. The steel comb is chiefly employed for streaking artificial oak, and the mottler is used for variegating and uniting the shades and tints of mahogany. Flannels and sponges are often worked with instead of brushes, but the implements most serviceable for veining or engraining purposes are small badger sash tools and sable pencils.

The effect produced by a coat of stain cannot be accurately ascertained until it has been allowed sufficient time for drying, and this allowance is most conducive to the development of nearly all external coatings.

SIZING AND EMBODYING.

The processes and manipulations of "pore-closing" and "hole-filling," which are soon acquired by a little attention and practice, cannot be too highly recommended to the polisher's notice as being most essential to the speedy development of a clear, smooth, imporous ground, which is the main object to be studied in French polishing.

It is found that plaster of Paris, when converted into a creamy paste, with water, proves a most valuable pore-filling material. It is to be rubbed, by means of a coarse rag, across the woody fibre, into the holes and pores, till they be completely saturated, and then the superfluous stucco on the outside is to be instantly wiped off. The succeeding processes are technically termed papering, oiling, and embodying.

When finely-pounded whiting is properly slaked with painters' drying oil, it forms another stuff and labor-saving pore-filler. It is applied in the same manner as the preceding one, and it is recommended on account of its quickly-hardening and tenacious virtues as a cement. Sometimes white lead is used in lieu of the whiting.

Before using either of these or other compositions for the same purpose, I generally tint them to correspond exactly with the color of the article I intend to size.

Holes and crevices may be well filled up with a cement that is made by melting beeswax in combination with resin and shellac.

A few expert artisans, who regard their modes of pore-filling as important secrets, do their work wonderfully quick, on one or other of the principles here described:—

1. After oiling, etc., they proceed to embody, keeping their rubbers in a sappy condition with thin polish, and taking special care to use no oil during this first stage of the polishing, which continues until all the pores are well closed. After having allowed their work sufficient time to harden, they smooth it with fine glass-paper, and embody it a second time with thicker polish, or a mixture of polish and varnish, causing their rubbers to work easily with half of the quantity of oil which is customarily employed. They afterwards rub this second body very smooth with moist putty.

2. Common work is first sized, then embodied, and then varnished; next, the outer coating is properly smoothed, after which the work merely requires a few rubberfuls of polish to make it ready for spiriting, *i. e.*, finishing.

3. I have often succeeded in filling some of the most spongy textures in this manner :—I wash them thoroughly, rubbing crosswise, with a sponge satu

rated with polish, till it becomes dry; then smoothing ensues; after which I proceed to embody them, employing stucco in the first embodying, and pumicestone in the second one. The mode of using either of these pounded substances, is to shake a few grains on the sole of the rubber when it is newly moistened with polish, then to cover the rubber with a fine linen rag, and to apply it in the ordinary way, observing, however, to put as little pressure upon it as possible. The stucco thus applied tends to fill up the pores and to harden the body of polish on the exterior; while the pumice-stone gradually diminishes all manner of roughness, and also helps to fill up the pores. Too much of the former should not be used, as it is apt to impart a semi-opaque appearance, and too much of the latter has a tendency to scratch the polished surface.

4. Comparatively few polishers have acquired so great a proficiency in the practice of the trade as to polish wood without altering, in a certain degree, its natural color. Here is an expensive system upon which any rich porous material, such as Italian walnut, can be made to take on a transparent gloss that will remain permanent for many years, and to retain the same tone of color after it is finished as it did before it was touched with any polishing liquid. The walnut receives a well-spread layer of refined glue, and after being permitted to become hard, the entire outer body of the glue is completely removed by the mechanical application of a steel scraper and glasspaper. Next, the woody fibre is twice embodied with white polish, and cleaned with scraper, etc. Lastly, proper sinking periods, smoothings with pumicestone, and slight embodyings with white polish, alternately succeed each other till the article is ready for the spiriting process.

In order to facilitate the necessary friction, a little purified grease ought to be used on the sole of the rubber instead of oil. The latter should never be employed for the polishing of an article that is only inlaid with walnut veneers, as, owing to their extreme thinness and porosity, the oil freely penetrates through to the ground wood, softening the glue, and causing the veneers to rise in blisters.

The gluey coating, which must be of precisely the same hue as the walnut, is seldom required for close-grained wood, like ebony and maple.

Superficial size is a transparent paste, which is suffered to remain on the exterior of large pieces of joinery and inferior cabinet articles that have been previously stained, and are merely to be varnished. It is sold by H. Stevens, London.

SMOOTHING.

There are numerous compounds and substances chosen for smoothing down the rough surface of coated woodwork; but in place of encumbering the present space with a long list of their names, I shall only specify the best materials, and give a brief explanation of the modes of applying them.

The outside face of bare woodwork simply requires to be papered, *i. e.*, scoured with glass-paper, which is papered in point of degree from No. 0 fine, to No. 3 coarse.

The operation of smoothing is admitted to be a most important branch of the art here treated of, for the obvious reason that, when it is judiciously conducted, it is ultimately found to contribute to two very desirable ends, namely, "full pores" and "smooth surfaces"

The roughness so peculiar to first coatings of varnish is nicely refined by being rubbed with No. 1 paper. Where the work is extremely coarse, it ought to be freely moistened with oil first, and then papered; under this treatment a thin paste is formed by the attrition, which not only reduces the grossness more effectually, but materially assists in filling up the open pores.

The process of refining second coatings, or more advanced bodies, is effected by rubbing them with a flannel thoroughly smeared with a paste formed of water and pulverized pumicestone.

Finely-pounded whiting, slaked with either oil or water, makes an excellent paste for refining bodies that are well advanced towards finishing.

Unctuous rust or incrustation is removed from the face of old bodies of polish, etc., by friction with a flannel smeared with a paste of Bath-brick dust and water. A strong lye of potash is frequently used for the same purpose; but I have discovered that the quickest and most effectual method of removing rust, is to scour it with pure spirit of turpentine; by this means the polish is preserved unsullied. Turpentine is also capable of neutralizing bodies of beeswax, etc.

When unadulterated spirit of wine is used in a tepid state, it washes off old coatings of French polish, spirit varnish, and lacquer.

Directions.

Let it be kept in remembrance that no job ought to be finished in the polishing, immediately after it has been smoothed, because the scratches occasioned by the use of glass-paper, or any of the pastes here specified, though imperceptible when the work is newly finished, become, in a short time afterwards, plainly discernible, causing the gloss to present an imperfect exterior.

Flat-surface work requires to be papered with a cork rubber, which is generally plied in the longitudinal direction of the grain.

In smoothing first coatings, and the more advanced bodies, rub the former transversely, and the latter circularly. Rub lightly and regularly; avoid cracking or scratching the outer face; and carefully deal with the edges and corners (of stained wood especially), as, by defacing or discoloring them, you will absolutely spoil the appearance of the work.

In the outset, the grain of ash, birch, or oak, can be mostly prevented from rising by sponging it with water, letting it dry, papering it, and at the commencement of the polishing process, by using the rubber only slightly moistened with thick polish or varnish, without oil, till the wood acquires a thin smooth skin; roughness can likewise be much avoided by strictly enforcing all the rules that are likely to promote cleanliness.

SPIRIT VARNISHING.

The brushes employed for this operation are the flat camel-hair ones. They vary in point of breadth from a quarter of an inch to four inches and upwards. The finest small white bristle tools and red sable pencils are found to be very serviceable for coating the delicately-shaped members, and the somewhat inaccessible cavities of turned and carved work. The way to preserve their elasticity is to rinse their hairy ends (after use) in finishing spirit; the spirit is then to be gently pressed out by passing the hair between the finger and thumb. After being cleaned, the brushes should be placed so as to hang perpendicularly, or to rest laterally within a dry air-proof vessel. Where these preservative principles have been neglected, the hardened brushes require to be soaked in the varnish for an hour or so, or if wanted for immediate use they can be softened in a few minutes by being steeped in lukewarm methylated finish. For several descriptions of fancy work, I prefer good Turkey sponges, as they are capable of spreading either stain or varnish more evenly than the camel tools.

The next thing worthy of notice is the varnish

dish, which ought to be a substantial earthen vessel, similar in size and shape to a small tea-saucer, but rather deeper, having two or three notches in its upper edge, to fit the handles of the brushes, the hairy ends of which should be kept lying on their sides—and not resting on their extreme points, as is commonly the case—while in the dish. The vessel should also have a "regulator" and a lid; the former consists of a piece of wire placed centrally across the mouth of the dish, and firmly fastened at both extremities; it is useful in regulating the proper quantity of stuff required in the coating tool at each dipping. A closely-fitting lid, when on, serves to keep the varnish free from dust, and other destructive agents, arising from constant exposure to the atmospheric air.

Rules.

Instantly after dipping, the brush or sponge is once or twice gently passed over the regulator; this prevents the tools from transferring an unnecessary quantity of polish to the work in operation. In merely putting on the first and second coats, the tool may be worked across the grain; but in finishing, it must be worked along the grain, and in either case the varnish must be equally and evenly laid on. In either sponging or brushing, the implement ought to be freely and lightly handled; it should also be plied with some degree of speed, as the varnishes of spirits have not the slow-setting properties which distinguish those of oil. Care should be taken to touch one part only once at a time, as by going over the same space twice, it is always rough on becoming dry. The most experienced varnishers maintain that it is best to make a sleek ground with a rubberful of French polish, always before the application of spirit varnish; and that it is equally important to dry the rubber thoroughly, leaving no degree of unctuousness upon the thin superstratum, previous to the laying on of a coat of finishing varnish. They unanimously assert, too, that it is of the utmost consequence in the production of a faultless gloss, to permit the last pellicle of polish to get an hour's rest before it receives a coat of fine varnish, and also to let the coating of slake "stand" for two hours prior to its being finally smoothed with a damp rubber.

FRENCH POLISHING.

SITUATIONS.—The ordinary difficulties attending the polishing of a fine article, which requires to be particularly well done, may be much lessened by having its various parts placed in an accessible position while it is being polished. The polishing shop should be a cleanly kept and commodious room, having good perpendicular windows, near each of which a bench ought to be situated. The most suitable benches— the tops of which are generally covered with thick soft cloths—are those measuring about six feet by three; and from three feet six inches to four feet in height. They must stand unfastened, so as to be removable at any time, in order to answer the different temporary positions in which the jobs require to be put. Before commencing to polish, I commonly place my work horizontally upon the bench, or upon a pair of pads on the floor, and I keep my face directly opposite the window while working. When, however, a perpendicularly-shaped specimen of cabinet ware, that requires to be operated upon in its erect attitude, comes under my treatment, I place it upon the bench, letting it rest on its feet or base, and while working, I stand between the bench and the window, keeping my back towards the latter.

RUBBERS.—The small pliable rubbers employed for doing carved framework, etc., are usually made of white wadding, and the large round ones used for surface work are mostly formed of soft flannel. The latter kind must be firmly made; and the more they possess such qualifications as proper size and solidity, the more quickly and satisfactorily will they polish extensive surfaces.

RAGS.—Fine linen makes the best rubber coverings and spiriting cloths, but cheap cotton will answer nearly as well. Both stuffs are preferred after having been used and washed several times. The way to wash them is, to boil them first in a strong lye of potash, and then in a weak one of soap powder, suffering each boiling to be succeeded by a thorough rinsing in clean water.

WETTINGS.—Some workmen wet the soles of their rubbers, by dipping into a saucer containing the preparation, and others by holding their bottles upside down, allowing the polish to shower through the drilled punctures of the stopples. Care should be taken not to soak the rubber too much by either means; and after wetting and covering, the sole ought always to be pressed forcibly upon the palm of the hand, so as to equalize the moisture.

RUBBINGS.—Invariably on beginning with a newly-wetted rubber, I gently and regularly sweep the surface from end to end in the running direction of the fibre, three successive times; I then rub across the grain with a semicircular motion, till the polishing tool becomes dry. This operation is of course repeated until the whole surface of the pores is no longer visible. The work so treated is now to be left in a clean apartment for a period of twelve hours; this being the time required for the complete absorption of the first body.

The sinking period having expired, the work is smoothed, dusted, etc., and then the polishing of it is recommenced. The first sweepings are similar to those described in the preceding embodying, after which I ply the rubber wholly with a rotatory movement, leaning lightly on it at first, and slightly increasing the necessary pressure towards the drying of it, which I finally accomplish by sweeping once or twice along the grain, expressly to remove any marks that may have been caused by the cross or round rubbings.

In these manipulations it is much better to use freely extended motions, than contracted ones; therefore the mechanical movements of the arm must on no account be confined.

RULES.—Wipe all the dust off your work at each recommencement. Allow every embodying a proper time to absorb and harden, previous to the reapplication of smoothing stuffs or polishes. Cover your rubber with a clean part of the rag at each wetting. Carefully guard against working your implement too long in one direction, and leaning too heavily on it when it is very wet, else you will be apt to produce coarse marks and streaky roughness.

Rubber marks may be removed by their being reversely rubbed with a heavily-pressed half dry rubber.

In polishing a very large surface, such as the top of a dining table, do only one-half at a time.

In spiriting, the finishing spirit should not be used in excess, because it dissolves a portion of the resinous or gummy body, and thereby causes dimness instead of brightness. If, however, the spirit be slightly mixed with polish, and be sparingly and judiciously employed, the desired clearness of lustre will make itself apparent. Prior to the application of the "spirit cloth," which consists of a few soft rags loosely rolled up in the shape of a large finger rubber and slightly damped with spirit, it is most essential to ply the rubber more quickly, and a little longer than ordinary, for the purpose of removing all signs of moisture and greasiness from the surface of the gloss.

Most polishers seem to think that nothing can be more productive of transparent brilliancy and durable hardness at the finish than the moderate use of spirit that has been somewhat weakened by exposure to the air, and an allowance of two hours as a resting period between the final embodying and the spiriting

DIRECTIONS FOR REPOLISHING.

In order to apply this process with facility, you will find it needful to disunite the various parts of each article. If your job be a wardrobe, take off the doors by unfastening their hinges; remove all the screw nails; take off the cornice; lift the wings or carcases from the base; and then separate the mouldings and other carved ornaments from the frames and panels of the doors. If it be a chest of drawers, pull the drawers out; unscrew the knobs or handles; remove the scutcheons from the key-holes; free the columns or pilasters from their recesses; and lift the carcase from off the base. If your job should happen to be a sideboard, separate the upper back from the top, unscrew the under back, and then take the base, top, and pedestals asunder.

After having disjoined the different portions and ornaments, take a pencil and put tallying marks on every two meeting sides; this will guide you in having everything appropriately replaced, when the complete article is finished.

The viscid rust must be thoroughly removed from the surface of the work; this is done by scrubbing it with a paste made of the finest emery flour and spirit of turpentine.

After cleansing, and before repolishing, it is a good plan to merely moisten the face of the work with raw linseed oil, for this causes the old body to unite with the new one.

Where shallow dents, scratches, and broken parts of the polish present themselves, carefully coat them two or three times with a thick solution of shellac, and when the last coatings become hard, rub them with soft putty until they become uniformly smooth and even then proceed to repolish the general surface.

GENERAL REMARKS AND USEFUL RECEIPTS.

Ornaments of brass must be well heated before they receive a coat of lacquer.

Equal parts of marrow oil, prepared ox-gall, and ivory black, all finely mixed, form a valuable composition for renovating old hair cloth.

After having been washed with spi.it of turpentine, and coated with colored varnish, old faded morocco looks almost as well as new.

Finely-varnished carved work presents a highly-polished appearance after it has been nicely smoothed with an oily flannel.

An elaborate piece of fine carving should go through the following process: 1st. It should be smoothly French polished to a good extent. 2d. Sponged or brushed with a thickish solution of shellac in spirit of wine. 3d. Minutely smoothed with the finest glass-paper; this is the most difficult process of all, and it requires assiduous and careful management. 4th. It should be again well embodied with polish, and then evenly coated with slake; the slaking must be done with care and precision. 5th. After hardening for a few hours, finish with a rubber slightly damped with thin polish.

Stains of ink are removed from writing desks, etc., by embrocation with oxalic acid, or spirit of salt. Stains that are purely alkaline can be neutralized with various soluble acids.

Slight indentations may be erased by repeatedly pressing wet pieces of paper upon them with a hot iron, till the moisture evaporates.

The approved mode of treating the top of a dining table, is to French polish it first, to glass-paper the polish off the surface, and then to polish it with oil.

Raw linseed oil is the only fixed oil used in French polishing.

French polish is made by dissolving twenty-eight ounces (avoirdupois) of shellac, and one and a half ounce each of sandrac, benzoin, and white resin. in a gallon of O. P. finishing spirit. By substituting pure bleached shellac for the ordinary brown kind, white polish is obtained.

The ingredients of common varnish are nearly similar to those of polish, but are somewhat different in their proportions, being forty ounces of shellac, four ounces of resin, five ounces of benzoin, two ounces each of sandrac and white resin, to the gallon of spirit.

Finishing varnish, which is distinguished by the technical name of slake, is prepared by dissolving an ounce of mastic and five ounces of benzoin in five gills of finishing spirit.

An excellent varnish for gilt work is compounded thus: Seedlac, in grain, 25 parts; gumlac, 30; gamboge, 45; annotta, 40; dragon's blood, 35; saffron, 30. The two lacs are mixed and dissolved in 130 parts of spirit of wine; this constitutes the varnish; the other ingredients are dissolved separately, each in 95 parts of spirit; these form the tinctures with which the varnish is colored to match the different shades of gold.

Brass lacquer is simply a solution of seedlac and gamboge in alcohol.

In the manufacture of each of the prescribed preparations, gums and resins are reduced to powder and put into a jar containing the proper quantity of spirit. The jar is kept in a hot bed of sand or water, and its contents are frequently agitated by shaking and stirring until they unite and form into a consistent liquid.

These fluids may afterwards be either thickened with gum or resin, or thinned with spirit of wine or rectified naphtha. They must always be carefully strained before use.

A deep blue dye is obtained by dissolving East Indian indigo in arsenious acid. Arsenite of copper produces a beautiful green; and here are directions for making another green stain: Digest a quantity of Roman vitriol in boiling water, to which add a similar quantity of pearl-ash, then forcibly agitate the mixture, and finish by gradually stirring into it a small allowance of pulverized yellow arsenic.

Clarified ox-gall both fixes and improves a great many colors; besides being useful as a mordant, it destroys unctuous matter; and when consistently used in varnishes, it prevents the coatings from cracking when they become old.

In slaking, a single coat is so very thin that it sometimes does not produce the desired effect; in such cases a second coat should be applied as soon as the first one becomes dry. It is an extremely bad plan to put slake on newly-spirited work, or to reapply it on old bodies.

The room in which polishing and varnishing are performed necessarily requires to be free from dampness; and its temperature must not fall below 45°, nor rise higher than 57° Fahrenheit.

Dexterous stainers can dye colorless timber in imitation of either rosewood or mahogany, with merely a strong decoction of logwood.

A deep scarlet stain is procured by macerating red sanders in rectified naphtha.

All use of the pastes and liquids which have hitherto been introduced and sold as "revivers," ought to be totally abandoned, because their properties have all been experimentally tested, and it is found that they prove more deleterious than beneficial; hence nothing is more successfully employed for both "polish-reviving" and "oil-polishing" purposes that raw linseed oil, moderately thinned with turpentine or spirit of wine.

The best method of preserving rubbers and sponges is to keep them in a close tin canister.

In the act of embodying or spiriting, the wet rubber should never be allowed to stick for an instant to the surface of the polish.

An effectual course of procedure in pore-filling is to make use of the usual quantity of oil, and to shake a small muslin bag containing smoothly-ground pumice-stone repeatedly over the job while it is being embodied. Dry plaster of Paris is frequently used in like manner.

Thin panellings for doors should be securely tacked down to a level board, with their fronts uppermost, and then polished with a large round flannel rubber having a very flat sole. But before fretted panels can be treated in that manner, their edges require to be entirely finished in the varnishing.

Of all the portions of furniture which come under the polisher's care, an elaborate fretting of rosewood is perhaps the most difficult to manage; this is not so much attributable to fibrous poriness as it is to the extreme delicacy and brittleness of the united members which form a complete panel or pediment. Indeed, to be successful in putting what is commonly called "a perfect gloss" upon the finer specimens of fretwork, patience and carefulness must constantly accompany industrious perseverance.

INDEX.

	PAGE
Anti attrition, to make	.134
Barometer scales, to silver	142
Beech, to stain a mahogany colour	66
Bedsteads, red stain for	68
Bone, to stain black	70
red	69
green	70
blue	70
yellow	70
Boxwood, to stain brown	72
Brass ornaments inlaid in wood, to polish	56
Brass figures, to wash over with silver	56
Brass-work, old, to clean for lackering	91
Brass, to imitate, in colouring	33
Bronze, do. do.	33
Bronzing, observations on	85
to bronze figures	85
brass figures for ornaments	87
Bronze, gold	97
copper	98
silver	98
tin	99
method of applying	99

INDEX.

	PAGE
Brushes for varnishing, to keep in order	106
Buhl-work, observations on	49
shell or brass-work, to prepare for cutting out	50
cutting out the pattern	50
gluing up the pattern	51
Cane chair-bottoms, to clean	135
to restore the elasticity of	135
Carpets, to clean	140
Cement, mahogany coloured	123
bank-note	123
turners'	124
for broken glass	124
to stop flaws in wood	125
for joining china	125
another	125
stopping, to make	151
Chairs, common red stain for	68
Chisels, and other edge tools, to temper	154
Crystallized tin	144
Clock faces, &c., to silver	142
varnish for	143
Cloth, to remove oil or grease from	138
wax-spots from	139
Clouds, to imitate in colouring	35
Colouring, rudiments of	31
Composition ornaments for picture-frames, &c	140
Compound lines and forms, for practice in drawing	19
ornaments and scrolls	20
Crimson curtains, to imitate in colouring	34
Drawing, first essay in	18
Drawing, rudiments of, as applicable to articles of furniture	13

INDEX.

	PAGE
Drapery, buff-coloured, to imitate	34
chintz do. do.	34
Drapery, white, to imitate	34
Dyeing wood, observations on	57
the kinds best suited for	57
Friction varnishing, or French polishing, observations on	117
French polish, the true, to make	118
another	119
improved	120
to remove dirt or grease from	152
Furniture, to varnish	105
old, to clean and polish	122
to take bruises out of	133
paste, to make	136
another method	136
oil, to make	137
another method	137
Geometrical terms explained and defined	21
drawing, definition of	13
Gilding, observations on	73
requisites necessary for	74
size for oil-gilding	74
for preparing frames	75
preparing frames or wood-work for	75
to polish for	76
gold-size for	77
preparing frames, &c., for	77
laying on the gold	78
burnishing	79
matting, or dead gold	80
finishing	80

INDEX.

	PAGE
Gilding, burnishing gold-size	83
Gilding metal, by dissolving gold in aqua-regia	146
Glass-paper	129
Glue, hints in melting and using	149
strong, for inlaying, &c.	48
for inlaying brass, &c.	56
Glues to resist moisture	126
Gluing, as applicable to veneers in table-tops, book-case fronts, &c.	46
Green baize, to imitate in colouring	33
Gilt poles, do. do.	34
Glass, do. do.	33
Ground, do. do.	35
Grass, do. do.	35
Grease, to remove from cloth	138
Green paint for garden stands, &c.	148
Gums, directions for choosing	104
Horn, to stain in imitation of tortoise-shell	69
to polish	116
to solder or weld	140
India japanning, observations on	94
ground for Chinese japan	95
black japan, to make	96
to trace the design	96
to raise the figures	96
gold bronze for	97
copper bronze	98
silver bronze	98
tin bronze	99
Inlaying with shaded wood	53
with silver strings, to imitate	54
Ivory, to stain red	69

	PAGE
Ivory, to stain black	70
green	70
blue	70
yellow	70
to polish	115
to soften	139
to bleach	139
to silver	146
Japanning, observations on	92
to prepare colours for	92
bronzes adapted for	97
black japan	93, 96
black rosewood, to imitate	93
work-boxes, &c	100
Jasper, to clean	135
King, or Botany-Bay wood, to imitate by staining	68
Lackering, observations on	88
brass-work	88
gold lacker for brass	89
another lacker	89
superior lacker	90
pale gold-lacker	90
lacker with spirits of turpentine	90
work in brass furniture, to clean	150
Leather, to gild, for bordering of doors, screens, &c	83
for border of library-tables, &c	84
Liquid for brightening and setting colours in dyeing wood	61
Liquid foil, for silvering glass globes, bent mirrors, &c.	82
Looking-glass, to clean	147

184 INDEX.

	PAGE
Mahogany, to imitate in colouring	32
to clean the face of	130
work, to clean and finish	130
light, to darken	131
to take ink-spots out of	136
Marble, to clean	135
to imitate in colouring	33
porphyry, to imitate in colouring	32
Sienna, do. do.	33
Mona, do. do.	33
black do. do.	34
to polish	116
Mirrors, to clean	147
Moulding, to resemble wood, to cast	150
Mountains, to imitate in colouring	35
Musical instruments, to stain a fine crimson	71
purple	71
black	71
blue	72
green	72
bright yellow	72
brown	72
Oil, spots of, to remove from cloth or silk	138
Ormolu, to imitate in colouring	33
Ornaments for cabinet-work, directions for drawing of	18
their terms explained	36
when and where most applicable	38
Ornaments, of what composed	36
foliage	36
mixed	36
festooned	37
arabesque	37
winding	37

	PAGE
Ornaments, serpentined, or running	37
plaited	37
guilloche	38
fret	38
mosaic	38
buhl	38
Ornaments most appropriate for hall-chairs	39
library-chairs	39
drawing-room chairs	39
card-tables	39
library and writing-tables	40
dining-tables	40
drawing-room tables	41
sofas	41
ottomans	41
dressing-table, or toilette	41
window-seats	41
cheval dressing-glasses	42
sideboards	42
cot-bed	42
bedsteads	43
drawing-room window drapery	43
libraries	43
fire-screens	43
to resemble wood, to cast	15
Ormolu ornaments, to clean	147
Parchment, to render transparent	138
Paste for laying cloth or leather tops	127
Perspective terms explained and defined	21
Perspective drawing, definition of	13
illustrated by diagrams and experiments	19
Pictures, to clean	141
another receipt	149

INDEX.

	PAGE
Plaster figures, to render durable	144
Portable glue	123
Porphyry, to clean	135
Plates, illustrative of cabinet and upholstery work—	
Plate 1, simple lines and forms	19
" 2, simple and compound do.	19
" 3, compound ornaments and scrolls	19
" 4, compound ornaments and scrolls	20
" 5, examples of perspective	20
Polishing, observations on	113
varnish	114
French, method of	114
brass ornaments inlaid in wood	115
ivory	115
any work of pearl	115
marble	116
Polish, French, to make	118
water-proof, to make	120
bright, to make	121
strong, to make	122
for turner's work	134
prepared spirits for, to make	121
Polished surface, to renew	149
Prints, figures of, to make appear in gold	112
Purificatory process before dyeing wood	57
Rivers, to imitate in colouring	35
Rosewood, to imitate in colouring	32
staining	67
Satin-wood, to imitate in colouring	33
Saws, to sharpen and set	132
Scagliola, to clean	135
Shadowing, rudiments of	28
Shell-gold, to make	81

INDEX.

	PAGE
Silvering	81
observations on	78
Silver furniture, to clean	135
size, to make	81
Simple lines, for first practice in drawing	18
Silk, to remove oil or grease from	138
wax spots from	139
Sienna marble, to clean	135
Sky, the, to imitate in colouring	34
Solid work, to clean the surface of	149
Spirits of wine, directions for choosing	104
Stippling, how to perform	30
Staining wood, observations on	65
Stain, to improve the colour of any	68
Steel-scrapers, good, to cut	132
Tables, to remove stains from	149
Tapestry, to clean	140
Tools, directions in the choice of	152
to temper	154
Tortoise-shell, to veneer	48
to imitate on copper	56
to polish	116
to solder or weld	140
Tracing paper, to make	145
Trees, to imitate in colouring	35
Varnishing, observations on	102
Varnish, sealing-wax	101
cautions respecting the making of	103
directions for choosing gums and spirits for	104
white-hard, to make	106
mastic, for pictures, &c	107
turpentine	107

INDEX.

	PAGE
Varnish, for violins	107
for drawings or card-work	108
another and better method	108
amber	109
oil	109
copal	110
colourless copal	110
turpentine copal	111
for prints, &c., stands water, and shines like glass	112
for prints, to resemble oil	113
to polish	114
prepared spirits for	121
for clock faces	143
Velvet, to imitate in colouring	33
Veneering, observations on	45
as applicable to card and other tops, &c.	46
Veneer, in buhl-work, to lay	52
Veneers, old, to raise and relay	47
Veneered surface, to clean	152
Verd antique, to imitate in colouring	33
Water, to imitate in colouring	35
Water-proof polish	120
Wax, black, to make	137
green, do.	138
spots to remove from cloth	139
Window curtains, to imitate in colouring	34
Winding foliage, of what composed	37
Wood, to bronze	86
Wood, to dye a fine black	58
blue	59
yellow	60
bright yellow	61

		PAGE
Wood, to dye a fine bright green		61
green		62
bright red		62
purple		63
orange		64
silver gray		64
gray		65
Wood, to stain a fine black for immediate use		66
beech a mahogany colour		66
another black		66
in imitation of rosewood		67
king or Botany-Bay wood		68
red, for bedsteads, &c.		68
Wood, porous, to clean the face of		130
to preserve from fire		148

INDEX TO APPENDIX.

	PAGE.
Alkaline fluids, use of	158
Antique hues of old oaks	156
Artificial graining, improving	159
Ash, to imitate oak with	161
Beech imitation	160
Beech, to imitate walnut with	163
Beech imitations	160
Birch, to imitate walnut with	163
Black stain	160
Blue dye, a deep	177
Brass lacker	176
Brass ornaments, lackering	175

	PAGE.
Brown stain	160
Brushes used in spirit varnishing	169
Cement for pore filling	165
Colors, to fix	177
Darkness	157
Dining table top, to treat a	176
Dyed polishes and varnishes, uses of	160
Ebony color	156
Ebony, discolored, improving	159
Ebony, to imitate	163

INDEX.

Elmwood in imitation of walnut 161
Embodying and sizing 164

Fine carving, to French polish 175
Fir, to imitate walnut with 163
French polishing 171
French polish, to make 176

Graining, artificial, improving 159
Grounding 156

Haircloth, composition for renovating 175
Hole filling 164
Honduras mahogany, improving 159

Imitations 160
Improving 158
Ink stains, to remove, from writing desks 175

Lacker, brass 176
Light yellowish woods, tones of 156

Mahogany color 156
Mahogany color, imitation 160
Mahogany, improving 159
Mahogany stain 162
Mahogany, to imitate, with logwood dye 177
Maple, improving 159
Matching of woods 157
Morocco, to renovate 175

Oak, old 156
Oak wainscot, imitation 161
Oil polishing 178
Old oak 156

Painting 159
Panelings, thin, polishing of 178
Plaster Paris for pore filling 164
Polishes and varnishes 160
Polishing shop 171
Polish, reviving 178
Pore closing 164
Pore filling 178

Rags for French polishing 172
Raw linseed oil in French polishing 176
Red stain 160
Repolishing 174
Revivers 177
Rosewood colors 156

Rosewood, improving 159
Rosewood, to imitate 162
Rosewood, to imitate, with logwood dye 177
Rosewood, to polish 178
Rubbers and sponges, to preserve 178
Rubbers for French polishing 171
Rubbings in French polishing 172
Rust, viscid, removal of 174

Satin wood stain 162
Scarlet stain 177
Size, superficial 167
Sizing and embodying 164
Slacking 177
Slake 176
Smoothing 167
Spirit cloth 173
Spirit varnishing 169
Spiriting in French polishing 173
Sponges and rubbers, to preserve 178
Staining, directions for 163
Staining wood 156
Stephens, Henry, compositions of 162
Stephens's satin wood stain 161
Superficial size 167

Thin panellings, polishing of 178

Varnish carved work, to oil 175
Varnish dish 169
Varnish finishing 176
Varnish for gilt work 176
Varnish, ingredients of 176
Varnishes and polishes, dyed 160
Varnishing room 177
Varnishing, spirit 169

Wainscot, oak 156
Walnut color 156
Walnut, dark, to imitate 163
Walnut, imitation of 161
Wash color 156
Washing 156
Wettings of rubbers 172
White lead for pore filling 165
Whiting for pore filling 165
Wood staining 156
Woods, imitations of 156
Woods, matching colors of 157

Yellowish woods 156
Yellow stain 160

BIBLIOLIFE

Old Books Deserve a New Life
www.bibliolife.com

Did you know that you can get most of our titles in our trademark **EasyScript**™ print format? **EasyScript**™ provides readers with a larger than average typeface, for a reading experience that's easier on the eyes.

Did you know that we have an ever-growing collection of books in many languages?

Order online:
www.bibliolife.com/store

Or to exclusively browse our **EasyScript**™ collection:
www.bibliogrande.com

At BiblioLife, we aim to make knowledge more accessible by making thousands of titles available to you – quickly and affordably.

Contact us:
BiblioLife
PO Box 21206
Charleston, SC 29413

Printed in Great Britain
by Amazon